"Sorry to break in on your recreation, fellows," the computer announced contritely, "but it **is** time for Sergeant Pinback to feed the alien."

Pinback groaned. "I don't wanna do that now."

"May I remind you, Sergeant Pinback," the computer continued inexorably, "that it was your idea in the first place to bring the alien on board. If I may quote you, you said, 'the ship needs a mascot.'"

"Yeah, but—" Pinback tried to protest. The computer rode over any objections.

"It was your idea, so looking after it is your responsibility, Sergeant Pinback."

Pinback walked off down the corridor muttering to himself. He reached the compartment they had sealed off for the live alien specimens. Over the door was a crude sign that read **Watch It!** The admonition had firm foundation in previous happenings, so he opened the door carefully.

His particular pet alien had grown more and more adventurous as it had become acclimated to the ship. The last time he had gone to look after it, it had been waiting just inside the door, ready to pounce on him . . .

Also by Alan Dean Foster
available now from Ballantine Books:

DARK STAR

Alan Dean Foster

Adapted from a script by
Dan O'Bannon
and
John Carpenter

A Del Rey Book

BALLANTINE BOOKS • NEW YORK

DARK STAR

Starring:	Dan O'Bannon
	Brian Nacelle
	Dre Pahich
	Cal Kuniholm
Written by:	Dan O'Bannon
	John Carpenter
Produced and Directed by:	John Carpenter
Executive Producer:	Jack H. Harris
Music by:	John Carpenter
Special Effects by:	Dan O'Bannon

Released by Jack H. Harris Enterprises, Inc.

"Auprès de ma blonde,
    qu'il fait bon, fait bon, fait bon.
Auprès de ma blonde,
    qu'il fait bon dormir . . . !"

1

Talby was counting stars again.

He didn't remember exactly when he'd lost count. Probably they were all noted down somewhere neat and official in the astronomer's records—or had he disconnected the tracker? It was hard to recall. There seemed to be something about uncoupling all the scientific instruments a while back, uncoupling them because it seemed blasphemous for such splendor to be reduced to a mere listing in a book.

Anyhow, the number didn't matter, did it? There were plenty of stars to go around, and if the muddlers back on Earth wanted records of them, let them come out here for themselves and do their own tracking. Talby didn't see how anyone could appreciate a star by using mere mathematical charts.

But he kept counting. It was easy. It was natural. It made a man free—one star, two stars, and baby makes three.

With only the naked eye, most navigators could distinguish only a few degrees, magnitude, but Talby had had more practice than most navigators. And he lived his work.

To get really good at it, you had to spend long stretches in practice, sharpening your perception and senses until eyes and mind operated instinctively. How could a man take the measure of a sun if he had to stop and think about it? Talby smiled.

He leaned back in the pneumatic astronomer's lounge, a pale bean in a pod of smooth maroon, and stared up through the dome. He'd buffed down the inside and outside so many times that the dome was almost impossible to see. Every imperfection had been scrubbed out of it, till now there seemed to be no dome. Only Talby and his seat, floating in a hole on the top of the ship.

Now and then the soft touch of a finger initiated a muted hum of precision machinery. The chair would swivel 90, 180, 270 degrees, and another section of the cosmos would come under Talby-scrutiny.

Five, six, pick up sticks.

Talby could distinguish almost *every* order of magnitude now. Of course, when the stars were your best friends, you didn't have to work very hard to find out about them. You didn't even have to ask. They told you and were happy to, confessed all their secrets without prodding, without coercion, without being violated by clumsy, poking, grabby machines.

That was the trouble with man's first extended explorations of deep space. He'd gone at it as he had gone at everything else throughout his history—hacking and clubbing and chopping, an ax in one hand and a scythe in the other. Never a moment to listen, to look, to try to see and understand. It was sad.

And it was so easy not to make the same old mistakes over again! If only they would try it his way, if only he could make them see. Talby shook his head, though there were none but the stars to see it. Useless. They wouldn't listen. They *never* listened.

Better to do it this way. At least he offended no one. At least one man had succeeded in blending with the universe without inflicting himself on it. And the universe repaid him in kind.

The others looked on his special relationship rather differently, of course. Poor middling souls—his greatest regret was that he couldn't share his pleasure with them.

Of them all, Doolittle came the closest to understanding, and even he insisted that the astronomer spent too much time up here in the dome, too much time alone, too much time staring into naked, empty space.

Empty space—poor, sad Lieutenant Doolittle! It was only empty *inside* the ship. They'd never understand that, either.

It had been only a few days, a few months, a few years. No doubt one day Doolittle might insist it had been too many centuries. It made no difference to Talby. He had accomplished the neat feat of dividing the universe into three parts: himself, the rest of the cosmos, and his fellow crewmembers. Doolittle, Pinback, Boiler, and Commander Powell.

No—no, that didn't sound right. There was something —oh, yes. Commander Powell had died. It occurred to him, as it sometimes did, that he should be forcing himself to make more of a contribution to ship life, to be more of a friend to the others.

He had trouble relating to them, though. Every day it grew harder. He tried comparing them to his real friends.

Let's see—Doolittle. Doolittle was an angry red giant, full of passion and fire and anger that blazed uncontrolled at unpredictable, unguarded moments. But he held the ship together, had done so ever since Powell had been eclipsed.

Boiler was a white dwarf, no reflection on his size. He was the largest of them, and the smallest. The most intense and the least demonstrative. The likeliest to collapse or go nova. His name fitted.

And there was Pinback—Pinback, the average, ordinary, down-home G-type lightbulb. Cheerfully pathetic Pinback, always joking, never laughing, barely noticed. And, like a sol-type star, he supported more life than the rest of them put together.

His mind shifted to muse on another G-type star, one he remembered fairly well, with a certain inconsequential world sputtering lazily around it.

He remembered that at one time he had lived on that world, that he probably (though it could not be verified without records) had been born on it.

A finger touched and made a hum—forty-five degrees more of infinity filled his gaze. This old man, he played seven, he played seven's and's gone to Heave—

There, in the upper quadrant of the Deeps—that looked like a binary. Of course, at this distance and using only the unaided eye it was quite impossible to tell a true double star from two stars that looked close together but were actually a thousand light-years apart.

Talby smiled slightly again. He *knew*.

For a moment he considered notifying Doolittle and the others of his discovery. They liked binaries.

No, they wouldn't be pleased. The rest of the crew was only interested in planets. At least, Boiler and Doolittle were. Pinback was interested in everything without being interested in anything.

But the other two—they liked planets well enough. Habitable ones first of all and then unstable ones that might make the others uninhabitable at some unseen future time. Lately he felt that Doolittle in particular was growing more and more fond of the unstable ones, and that bothered Talby for reasons he couldn't pin down.

Insignificant, germ-ridden dust specks—planets. Inconsequential motes, fungi on the skin of the galaxy. He tilted the chair more steeply and stared smugly outward.

Let Doolittle and Boiler and Pinback have their moldy little worlds. He, Talby, existed in perfect oneness with the stars themselves. How could he bring himself to notice anything as minute as a mere planet?

Oh, there were other things big enough to interest him. Occasional nebulae—delicate, pretty, but insubstantial. The infrequent aberrations, like black holes, were unaesthetic.

Let Doolittle and the others think what they might about him; he wasn't troubled. He would stay civil no matter what dark thoughts they voiced. Let them think anything they liked so long as they kept the ship running efficiently for him.

For that was how the head astronomer of the *Dark Star* had come to think of it. He was no longer a component of the ship—rather, the ship existed to support him. He sighed in perfect contentment.

As long as the others left him alone to commune with his friends, the stars, he was happy. The motionless myriad suns were companions enough for him. The suns, and perhaps, someday, the Phoenix.

Nine, ten . . . begin again.

Sergeant Steel held on to his guts as he stared at the approaching Goering Panzer. The ring of the grenade was clamped bitterly in his sweating teeth. He had one chance for the platoon. Get up and ram that egg down the Panzer's open hatch before her 88mm. and twin machine guns could spit death among his trapped men. He steeled himself for the leap—

The communicator buzzed for attention. Pinback reluctantly put down the tattered issue of *Real War Stories* —*Action Comics* and stared at the switch set in the wall. For a moment he thought the buzzing had stopped. He returned to the busy Sergeant Steel, but the nasty instrument interrupted again.

He was forced to acknowledge.

Doolittle's voice was mildly peeved. "Pinback, if you can tear yourself away from improving your mind, we could use you forward. We're getting close."

"Aw, I'm just getting to the good part, Doolittle."

"You've read every one of those comics at least thirty times, Pinback," responded the lieutenant tiredly. "Get your ass forward."

"Oh, all right!" Pinback snapped off the intercom and lovingly marked his place in the magazine.

Darn Doolittle anyhow, he muttered to himself as he ambled forward. So they had another sun to blow, so what? It wouldn't have hurt to let him finish the book. Sometimes Doolittle really got on his nerves.

As usual, no one said anything to him when he walked into the narrow bridge–control room. Slipping mutely into his seat between Doolittle and Boiler, he made a casual check of the readouts, nodded to himself.

Uh-huh, sure enough. They had lots of time before coming in drop range of the target luminary. Doolittle just wanted to irritate him by bringing him forward early. Well, he wasn't going to let it show.

Then he noticed the tell-tale flashing idly at the base of his communications grid. It was the deep-space receive. He looked right at Boiler, then left at Doolittle. Their tell-tales were flashing too, yet neither man seemed to notice, or care. No telling how long they'd been flashing.

He activated the grid and the computer voice promptly announced, "Attention, attention. Incoming communication from Earth Base, Mission Control, McMurdo Sound, Antarctica. To *Scout Ship Dark Star*."

Dazed, Pinback stole another glance at his companions. Still, no one seemed the least bit interested. Well, they weren't going to get a rise out of him. So he ignored the computer also, while the message continued to repeat.

One man was a crowd on the narrow bridge. With the three of them it was intolerably close, and highly efficient.

But there were other reasons why the bridge was so small. One was that many sections of the ship, now empty, had once been packed with compressed acres of food, spare parts, and living material—most of which was now gone.

And there had to be lots of room for the bombs. It bothered Pinback that Doolittle and Boiler persisted in calling them bombs. He always tried to get them to refer to them by their proper names—thermostellar triggering devices.

But Doolittle persisted in calling them bombs. The term seemed inadequate to Pinback for such a godlike and overwhelming concatenation of modern technology. Once in a while Boiler would call them something else, usually unmentionable, because the bombs were the main reason they were on this unmentionable mission.

Talby didn't call them bombs, but then Talby didn't

refer to them at all, Of course, Talby was crazy anyway, so it didn't much matter. But that bothered Pinback too, because Talby didn't look crazy, or sound crazy. The alternative was that Talby was sane and the rest of them were crazy. Pinback found this line of thought unpleasant, and he dropped it.

Now Commander Powell, he'd *always* called them thermostellar triggering devices, but Commander Powell was—

"Attention, attention. Incoming communication from Earth Base, Mission Control, McMurd—"

The tension was too much for Pinback. Phooey on Boiler.

"Hey, guys," he said finally, his voice the usual combination of half pleading, half whine. "It's a message from Earth. All the way from Earth. Isn't anybody going to acknowledge it?"

Boiler's reaction was predictable. He just lay back in his chair, punching alternating buttons. The buttons didn't do anything. Nobody could remember what the buttons used to do. But punching them didn't affect the ship, so Boiler kept doing it. One on, one off. One on, one off.

Boiler was always punching things lately, not always inanimate things, either. Pinback liked Boiler even though the big sandy-haired gentleman hated the sergeant's guts. Pinback liked everybody. It was the best thing about him, really.

So he kept trying to make friends with Boiler. When Boiler made it particularly hard on him, Pinback rationalized that it was his contribution to maintenance of the ship's morale. The task was necessary, then, for the good of the ship as well as for the good of Pinback. Secretly, deep down, what he really wanted to do was see Boiler reduced to his component atoms. And he kept it deep down, because he was afraid of Boiler. He had no question in his mind, no question at all, that Boiler could beat him to a pulp anytime he felt like it.

Pinback returned his attention to Doolittle, tried to put a mite more grit into his voice, and failed miserably.

"Lieutenant Doolittle, sir, aren't we going to accept the message? Sir?"

Doolittle looked back at him with that faintly contemptuous air he seemed to reserve for Pinback alone. "Message? Why bother? They wouldn't have anything important to say. And they never have anything *nice* to say. So why bother?

"Besides, we've got an unstable world coming up, Pinback. Or have you forgotten already? You could have, you know. You're particularly good at forgetting things, Pinback."

There! Now why did he have to go and say a thing like that? Pinback tried to ignore it.

"I know that, sir. I know we've got another unstable world to blow. And I'm ready for it, sir, ready as always —but a message from Earth! We haven't had a message from Earth in, well, in days, sir."

"Months," mumbled Boiler.

"Years," corrected Doolittle.

Pinback was discouraged. He badly wanted to hear that message. But should he acknowledge it by himself? Wasn't that kind of a bold step?

Why should it be? He outranked everyone on the ship now except Doolittle. That is, he would have outranked everybody on the ship except Doolittle if he were Sergeant Elmer Pinback, Deep Space Exploration Forces. But he wasn't Sergeant Elmer Pinback—or was he?

If he wasn't Sergeant Elmer Pinback, then, who was he? What was it Doolittle had said about forgetting? No, no!

He looked down at his uniform and sighed with relief. The name sewn into his jersey definitely said *Pinback*. And that was the only name he could think of for himself, though there was a tiny door opening in his mind, just a crack, that—

He slammed it shut. He was Sergeant Elmer Pinback, Deep Space Exploration Forces, and that was about enough nonsense!

As it developed, he was spared the need to make a decision, which pleased him greatly. He didn't like making decisions. He wasn't very good at it and he never would be very good at it.

Doolittle didn't like making decisions either, but it seemed to come naturally to him. Oh, the lieutenant didn't have any flair for it, and he didn't do it with much conviction—not like Commander Powell, say. But Pinback didn't care so long as *he* didn't have to do it.

Doolittle reached out a hand and lazily flipped the Receive switch.

The main screen over their heads started to clear. Pinback looked up at it anxiously, hopefully. Maybe, maybe it was even a recall order. He chided himself. That was a damn silly thought. There would be no recall order until they had finished their mission.

But it didn't hurt to hope.

Doolittle's eyes inclined easily upward, and after a while so did Boiler's—out of boredom, no doubt. A pause while the computer untangled, realigned, and enhanced the last of the high-beam, extreme-long-range communiqué. Then the screen cleared and an alien appeared in the middle of it.

The alien had a wide pink face with unbearable pale pink skin. The rest of it was clad in a snug-fitting, freshly pressed uniform. It had two blue eyes, a divided nose, a mouth with the normal complement of teeth—now broadened into a wide smile—and was no older then anyone on board the *Dark Star*. This made it look no less impossibly young, and innocent. It was also cleanshaven and closely cropped on top, which made its face look obscenely naked. The alien was a human being.

The crew of the *Dark Star* had all been human beings once upon a time. Exemplary human beings. A quintet of the most accomplished young human beings in existence. But they had all changed somewhat since that last, glowing evaluation had been made.

They'd been chosen partly because of their youth. Because of it—for although they might be away from Earth for only five or ten years shiptime, a century or so would pass back on their home world.

It was felt that young men returning still young from

such an ordeal would be better able to adapt to whatever new society and civilization they found than would middle-aged men returning old. Also, the younger the man, the more resilient his emotions, the faster his reflexes—and the less he would have to remember and be sad about. Or so the psychometricians had argued.

They were partly right, and partly wrong. The men of the *Dark Star* did have less to remember than older men would have. But they remembered it that much more strongly.

So they looked into the mirror that was the communications screen and watched while this pale alien organism jabbered meaninglessly at them and they hated it and all that it now represented.

It was harder for Doolittle. Talby had his stars, and Pinback his almost-memories and his comic books, and Boiler his silent anger—but Doolittle had only memories, held stronger than most. So he hated it most of all.

Hated the hot bath the man had clearly enjoyed not too long ago. Hated his pleasant smile and honest good nature. Hated his clean clothes and polished epaulets and fresh air, and most especially he hated the girl the man was probably going to meet that night after they finished preparing this broadcast, hated the smooth thighs and fine soft belly and geometrically luscious . . .

He hated the computers he could see whirring mindlessly behind the man, and the men who ran those computers, and the computers who ran those men and their wives and their wive's friends, and the friends of the wive's friends and the buddies they played golf with on Sunday, and the kids of the buddies they played golf with on Sunday, and the outings they all went on to the beach . . .

To the beach, the beacon of the world, the olive-green light that burned in the back of his pounding skull.

He hated them all—the taxpayers of the world who had heeded the fatuous exhortations of the scientists and politicians to make the habitable worlds of the galaxy safe for human colonization. Make them safe by funding the *Dark Star* project.

Make them safe by removing any unstable planetary bodies or oddball worlds that coexisted in a system with them. An eccentricity of orbit, an internal rumble of molten indigestion—that was enough to send the *Dark Star* homing in on a planet to plant a thermostellar trigger in its lower intestine, set off a chain reaction, and remove from it forever a chance to interfere with future human settlements. Most of all Doolittle hated them because they had been the ones ultimately responsible for putting him out here. And because they wouldn't let him return home until this run was finished.

Not that the crew of the *Dark Star* was untrustworthy, or not among the most stable of the race, no. But there was always the outside chance—just a hint, the psychometricians said—that even the best men could go bonkers on a trip of this length. So, to be on the safe side the *Dark Star* itself had built into its structure explosive material that could be rendered inert only when the last thermostellar device had been successfully dropped, as recorded by the computer. Then they would be permitted to return home to full honors and acclaim and due process.

But they couldn't chance letting one of those planet-busters back into Old Sol's backyard.

Still, they were almost finished. What had begun as a leisurely journey had turned into a frenzied search for yet another unstable world, and another. Eighteen unstable planets destroyed in three years, shiptime. Three years—twenty years back on Earth.

They were far ahead of the best estimates, but certain things even the psychometricians hadn't imagined could drive men to superhuman effort.

And now only two bombs were left, numbers nineteen and twenty; and once they were successfully launched on their suicidal way, the *Dark Star* could go home. Home . . . back to and among the aliens he hated.

Doolittle didn't remember exactly when he had started hating the pink-faced aliens. But then it struck him that he didn't remember a lot of things lately—ever since Commander Powell had died. He activated the start switch.

The alien coughed lightly, cleared its throat, and began smoothly, with only the slightest tinge of self-consciousness.

"Hi, guys," it said brightly. "Glad we got your message finally. You'll be interested to hear it was broadcast live over the whole Earth—in prime time. You should have seen the ratings, guys. I mean, it was phenomenal. Knocked the top-rated . . ."

The alien hesitated, as if he was listening to someone speaking out of hearing range. He nodded imperceptibly and spoke again, rather more solemnly now.

"About the first of the colony ships. Everyone in the U.N. had been haggling over it for months, but that message from you guys threw it all over to the pro-colonization forces. Nothing like some honest emotion to sway recalcitrant politicos. The brass here at Mission Control are real proud of the way you fellas conveyed real anguish and tears and all.

"They should be getting started on the actual construction of the first ships any day now. There are just a few last details to be ironed out. Like, the Soviets claim the deep-space drive is their invention so they should have the largest number of colonists, while the Chin . . . Chinese think that it should be loaded according to the percentage of world population.

"The Israelis are pushing for an extra-large allotment on their claim of having designed the computer; and we, of course, feel that since we paid for most of the hardware so far and supplied the crew, that we ought to have a few more than the Wops and the . . ."

Again the alien looked nonplussed, listening to someone off-mike. His smile reappeared easily a moment later.

"But that's all internal politics and needn't concern you guys and the wonderful job you're doing." He hesitated and looked slightly concerned. "The time lag on these messages is getting longer . . . even longer than the boys here in relativity computation had expected. We gather from the ten-year delay that you are approximately eighteen parsecs out. We anticipated originally, as you will recall, that you would work more of a circular course closer in to Earth. But I guess systems with habitable worlds and unstable ones in combination are farther apart than the boys here predicted, right?

"The upshot of what I'm trying to say is that some people here get nervous when we don't hear from you as frequently as scheduled. We know you guys have lots of things to do, but"—Boiler made a growling sound—"try and drop us a line a little more often, okay? Just to say hiya." His grin broadened weakly and he looked down at a cuesheet out of camera view.

"As to the specifics of your message—sorry to hear about the radiation leaks on the ship, but equally glad to hear they've only affected minor mechanisms and haven't touched anything basic to your mission. Really sorry to hear about the death of Commander Powell. I was personally all broke up. Of course, I never had the honor of actually meeting him, but I remember how we used to read about him and the rest of you wonderful guys in school. There was a week of mourning here on Earth. The flags were at half mast, and a Congressional inquiry has been launched to investigate the firm that made the defective seat circuitry.

"We are informed, though, that the seat circuit shorting out like that was a one-in-a-million chance, so the rest of you should have no compunctions about sitting down on the job, hah, hah." He smiled again.

"We're all behind you wonderful guys a hundred percent. The job you're doing now will be remembered by billions of successful colonists thousands of years in the future, when all those systems you've cleared are filled with flourishing new populations—all operating under democratic principles, we expect." He winked.

"Now, about your two requests . . ." His eyes strayed to the hidden sheet again.

"I hate him," Doolittle whispered under his breath.

"Gee, what a nice fella," Pinback grinned inanely. Boiler growled and punched buttons.

"First, about your request for portable radiation shielding and weld mechanism to replace the apparently defective plating." He shook his head. "Sorry to have to report that this request has been denied. I hate to send bad news when you guys are doing such a wonderful job, but I think you'll take it in the proper spirit." He heaved a theatrical sigh. "You know how politicians are when money is mentioned.

"There have been some cutbacks in the U.N. appropriations, and what with the cash for the colony ships and all having such a rough time getting through committee, we just can't afford to send a hyperspeed cargo shuttle out there to you. I've got to confess it didn't help our case when we had to admit that we didn't know exactly where you were, but have you ever tried explaining to a minister from Malaysia how big a parsec is?

"But I know you guys will make do. You've been doing amazing things so far. Lourdes—he's our project chief now, and a nicer, sweeter guy you couldn't find anywhere—says he doesn't know how you and Boiler got the shielding redistributed near the drive without getting a lethal dose of radiation. He doesn't *think* it made you sterile, since you should have died in the first place, but you guys shouldn't worry about that.

"About your other request." He leaned forward and looked right and left in a conspiratorial way. "Frankly, if it was up to me and the regulars here at Deep Space Mission Control, we'd cryostate the six girls and shoot 'em out to you. Only trouble was, some idiot leaked the request to the press, and they blew it up out of all proportion. But don't worry." He sat back and winked again. "We covered for you guys . . . made out how it was all a big joke on your part to show how well you're doing, right?"

Boiler was punching buttons faster now.

"Gee, what a nice fella," Pinback repeated, his smile a little less broad now.

I wish it were him up here and me down there smiling idiotically up at him, Doolittle thought desperately.

"So I'm really afraid," the alien continued, "that the request has been declared inoperative. But at least you know that we down here sympathize with you guys. It's the higher-ups who're making things tough."

"I'll bet he's queer as a two-dollar bill," Boiler said suddenly. "Flaming queen." Growl.

"He looks like a queer—look at his nails."

"That might be the current style on Earth," countered Pinback. "Anyway, you can't see his nails. They're below the vision pickup."

"Well, I saw 'em," Boiler insisted, his voice rising dangerously. He glared at the sergeant. "Wanna make something of it?"

"Well, gee, no," Pinback admitted. "I mean, it didn't seem to me it meant that much to you . . . I mean . . ."

"Goddamn faggots," Boiler rumbled.

"Quiet, Boiler," Doolittle said softly. He had his finger on the *Hold* button. "We've started it . . . we may as well hear all of it." As he lifted his finger off the control, Boiler lavished a last predatory glare on the subdued Pinback and returned to his button pushing. It didn't seem quite as much fun now. Damn queer had broken his concentration. Who needed their stupid messages anyhow?

"So anyway, that's how it is down here on Earth. Or up here on Earth, depending on which way you guys are heading, hah, hah. I wish there was something more I could say," and for a moment a flicker of humanity seemed to appear in the alien's face. Again he seemed to acknowledge the words of an off-screen presence, and the flicker disappeared.

"Well, as you know, these deep-space calls cost a lot of money, so all I can say for all of us here at McMurdo is, keep up the good work and drop us a line more often, huh?"

Fizzle . . . pop . . . the words END COMMUNICATION appeared on the screen. Doolittle switched it off.

"Surprised he didn't blow us a goodbye kiss," muttered Boiler. The other two ignored him.

Nice to know they're thinking about us so warmly, isn't it, guys?" Pinback ventured cautiously, looking from Doolittle to Boiler and back to Doolittle. "Isn't it?"

"Quiet, Pinback," said Doolittle, working controls. "We're almost there. We've got a planet to blow."

"Ah, gee, you guys never wanna talk anymore." Pinback folded his arms and sat back, pouting. "Blow it up, blow it up—that's all you think about anymore. We do that all the time. When was the last time we all just sat around and talked, huh? About nothing in particular?"

"You do that all the time, Pinback," Doolittle commented.

"Yeah, but it's pretty dull just talking *to* you guys if you don't chat back. I might as well talk to a blank wall."

"You do that all the time, Pinback."

Oh, you think you're so smart, Doolittle, Pinback muttered silently. Always ready with the snappy comeback, aren't you? Well, we'll see who comes out of this mission with a clean bill of health! Wait till the psyche boys get a look inside *your* head. Then you'll be sorry you didn't talk to me when you had the chance.

I tried to help you, Doolittle, but you don't want to be helped, so don't blame me when they lock you in solitary for observation, with doctors poking and monitoring and prodding and digging into your brain, digging, digging . . .

Pinback was glad when Doolittle switched the overhead screen from communications to fore visual pickup. He was beginning to drown in the sweat of his own thoughts.

A world sprang into sharp focus. It was sterile, empty, deserted. No animals moved on its surface, no fish swam in its seas. Nothing grew and nothing moved. It was no different from a thousand other worlds they had encountered, but it had one thing in common with eighteen others—eighteen others they had encountered and destroyed.

They had found two habitable worlds in this system. One planet was very Earthlike, the other marginally so. Some day each might support a population as great as that of Earth's today.

But as things stood there would be no point in planting an incipient civilization on either of them because this world, according to computer predictions, sat in an unstable orbit. In not more than two hundred thousand nor less than five thousand years it would spiral inward to intercept its own sun.

There was the chance that nothing serious would happen—the world might be turned instantly to ashes. However, if conditions were right, it could be enough, just enough, to alter the position of the star in relation to its habitable planets. Or worse yet, set it on the path to nova.

Waste it, and want not, Doolittle thought—the motto of the scientists who had proposed and organized the *Dark Star* mission and its objectives.

So now they would commence operations to quietly eliminate a world in a soundless, overwhelming explosion bigger than any ever seen on Earth, thereby rendering the system safe for Mom, Apple Pie, and another four or five billion of the social insect called man. A voice sounded in his earphones.

"What'd you say, Pinback?" he mumbled in reply. "*Goggle, freep, tweep.*"

He spoke into the mike again. "What was that? I still can't understand you." Might as well be nice to poor Pinback. After all, he tried his best to do a sergeant's job.

Pinback was always trying. That was one of his problems. At times he reminded Doolittle just a bit too much of the unctuous young officer who had delivered the message from Earth base.

One of these days Corporal Boiler was going to . . .

Pinback shoved the mike aside and leaned over. "I said, I'm trying to reach Talby. Something's wrong with the damned intercom. If you're not going to talk to me, then I'm going to work. I need a last-minute diameter

approximation. Do you expect me to figure that myself?"

"Calm down, Pinback. There's something wrong with
everything on this ship." He flicked a fingertip on his
own mike. "Talby, Talby, this is Doolittle, do you read
me? Answer me, Talby . . . wake up, man."

Eleven, twelve, thirteen, wonder what I've seen . . .
Three blue-white suns, just above the plane of the
ecliptic. He jotted them down in his mental catalog. Odd
to see three of the same magnitude grouped so closely
together. Another interesting surprise.

Exactly how many stars were now included in his private collection he didn't know. There were at least several thousand. He would know better if he entered them
formally in the ship's scientific records—something he
adamantly refused to do.

Doolittle had bugged him about it when he found out
what the astronomer was doing—or rather, wasn't
doing. But Talby's smile had defeated him. You couldn't
reduce a star to an abstract figure, Talby had patiently
tried to explain. It was demeaning, both to the man and
to the star. Doolittle gave up after a while.

Talby touched controls, and the observation chair
swerved another ninety degrees, tilted forward. Maybe
he could convince Doolittle to rotate the ship again, so
that he could see the other half of the heavens for a
while. Doolittle never understood these requests. He insisted that after a while all stars looked the same: uniform, ugly little fireflies glaring in the night-space. Talby
couldn't make him see. Poor Doolittle.

Poor Talby.

Something buzzed insistently in his head. At first he
thought it might be another of his headaches. In a way,
it was.

"Talby, Talby, this is Doolittle. Can you read me?
Acknowledge, Talby."

The corporal blinked, forced himself out of the real
universe and back into the irritating dreamworld of

reality . . . the triangular dreamworld of the *Dark Star*.

"Oh, yes, Doolittle. Yes, I read you. What is it?"

Doolittle continued to manipulate the instruments in front of him as he spoke to Talby. The astronomer was beginning to worry him. No, no . . . that wasn't quite right. Talby had been worrying him for some time now. He always meant to do something about it, but there were so many other things to worry about, so many other tasks he was responsible for now.

Not that Talby had ever done anything to threaten the safety of the ship—quite the contrary. He was efficient in his duties to the point of abnormality. But it bothered Doolittle that the astronomer spent so much time in the observation dome. It bothered Doolittle that Talby didn't eat his meals with the rest of them. It bothered Doolittle that Talby never joined them for their admittedly deadly dull group recreation periods.

But mostly it bothered Doolittle because Talby seemed so friggin' happy . . .

"Uh, Lieutenant Doolittle?" He blinked, glanced irritably at Pinback.

"I'm okay, Pinback. Hello, Talby? We need a diameter approximation here."

"Roger, Doolittle," responded Talby, prompt, efficient. "Have it in a minute."

"Talby, were you counting again?"

"I'm always counting, Lieutenant. You know that." A pause. Then, "Point zero niner five—no special setting required. Too bad it's a bummer."

"Yeah," said Doolittle curtly. "Thanks, Talby."

Doolittle would have liked to hate Talby. For his happiness, for his easy efficiency, for the way he stood the agony of the voyage. But he couldn't. Talby was one of them. Talby was human in a way the frog-faced messager from Earth never could be.

Pinback again. "I need a GHF reading on the gravity correction."

"I'll check it," Doolittle replied.

"I'll have a By SA plus one, Boiler."

Doolittle almost smiled. They were operating loose, easy now. The supersmooth crew of the *Dark Star* was doing what it had been trained for. Each man became an integral part of the unit, each subordinating his personal opinions, desires, and feelings to the overriding demands of the mission.

It was rather like making love. They could even think about that now without breaking down, when functioning as a team. Even think about se—No, no, that was one thought he still had to suppress. The psychometricians had felt they'd compensated adequately for that, but ever since the auto-erogenizer had broken down . . .

He checked a gauge. "Pinback?"

"Yeah, Doolittle."

"Your GHF reading is minus fifteen."

"Okay." Pinback did things with the controls at his station, frowned slightly.

"Doolittle?"

"Yeah."

"I need a," he hesitated, checked the readout, "a computer indication on a fail-safe mark."

"Roger, Pinback."

"Boiler, can you set me up with some overdrive figures?"

"Ninety-seven million less eight corrected for expected time critical mass."

"That checks out here." The sergeant nodded. "I have a drive reading of seven thou."

"No conflict. Systematization keyed and ready," Boiler replied easily.

Odd, Doolittle reflected, how harmonious Pinback and Boiler could be when operating together for the good of the mission. Maybe if all mankind could be involved in some similar, single project, where each needed the aid of his neighbor, they could function together like the sergeant and corporal.

It was only in the off moments—which meant all the

time they weren't actively engaged in running the ship
—that animosity flared between the two.

And himself, he was forced to add. Pinback could put
him off his mettle any time he opened his mouth. It
wasn't that the sergeant was trying to be obnoxious; he
just couldn't help himself.

Strange how the psyche boys could place Pinback in
the crew with him and Boiler and Powell. That produced a click in his mind and brought back unpleasant
thoughts which he quickly shoved aside. It bothered him
that he'd forgotten again.

All the more reason to drive themselves, loose the last
of the bombs, and start on their way home.

"I read that quantum increase of seven," Pinback was
saying.

"Pinback, I have that computer reading. It's nine-
five-seven-seven. Repeat, nine-five-seven-seven."

"Time to start talking," Boiler observed. The three
men leaned back in their lounges. There was a hum in
the control room. "Bomb-bay systems operation confirmed."

Two panels slid apart in the belly of the white arrow-
head that was the *Dark Star*. A long tube lowered from
it. Attached to its end was a thick disk holding a long,
rectangular box-shape. The box-shape had the number
19 painted on its sides.

It was born out of a computer relay from the *Dark
Star*'s brain and would die soon in a funereal conflagra-
tion unknown in this part of the galaxy till now. The
rectangular box-shape with the number 19 painted on its
sides was, as Pinback insisted, a thermostellar device—
or, as Boiler and Doolittle persisted, a bomb.

The sergeant reached up and flipped an overhead
switch. The words LOCK FAIL-SAFE appeared on the
screen in front of him.

"Fail-safe engaged." He tapped the end of his microphone and blew into it once. "Sergeant Pinback calling
bomb."

Doolittle gave him a look, but Pinback ignored it. He

couldn't see any harm in being convivial, even with a bomb.

"Bomb number nineteen, do you read me, bomb?"

The voice that replied was muted, relaxed, and not at all concerned about its impending suicide. "Bomb number nineteen to Sergeant Pinback. I read you, Sergeant. What's up?"

"Well, bomb," Pinback continued conversationally, examining his nails, "not much." There, that was pleasant enough. He 'tried to be this way with each bomb before it was dropped. After all, they didn't live very long. And no matter what Doolittle and Boiler thought, he felt bombs were pretty nice people—for planet-destroying machines, that is.

To be perfectly honest about it, he'd rather talk to one of the bombs than to Boiler any day.

"Well, bomb, it's just about sixty seconds to drop. Just wondering if everything is all right." He adjusted another set of controls. "How are you feeling?"

"As well as can be expected. I'm looking forward to carrying out the mission for which I was designed."

"Atta boy, bomb. Checked your platinum-iridium energy grid? And your shielding?"

"Grid and shielding positive function," the bomb replied good-naturedly.

"Swell," said Pinback. "Tell you what, bomb. Let's go ahead and synchronize detonation time. Ah, you wouldn't happen to know when you're due to go off, would you?"

"Detonation in six minutes, twenty seconds."

"Good, good. Just let me double-check that."

"Very well, Sergeant Pinback."

"All set here, bomb. We match up. Arm yourself."

A few small red lights flashed briefly from the back of the thermostellar device. That was all there was to indicate that the inert construct of metal and plastic was now the most dangerous single object within a hundred parsecs.

"Armed," it said sharply.

"Well then . . ." Pinback sighed, looked around for

something else to do. "Everything looks good, bomb. Dropping you off in about thirty-five seconds. Good luck."

"Thanks," said the bomb. Its diagramatic targeting computer had already locked on to the world below.

The interior of the control room now became a flurry of controlled activity as final preparations were made. Then Boiler and Doolittle sat back as Pinback gripped a pair of opposing knobs and stared at the small chronometer set into the panel above his station.

"Beginning primary sequence."

Doolittle flipped a last switch, watched a red light wink on in front of him.

"Sequence activated. Commence countdown."

"Roger. Mark it: ten, nine, eight, seven, six, five, four, three, two, one." Both switches were turned simultaneously. "Drop."

There was a bright flare of light from the point where the bomb contacted its release disk. The thremostellar trigger dropped away from the ship. The disk and tube were drawn rapidly up into its belly.

"Hyperdrive sequence begun," Doolittle noted. "Hit it, Pinback."

The sergeant hit a pair of buttons in rapid succession. "Force field activated . . . sequence engaged." He sat back in his chair. A slight tingle started to come over his whole body, as if his leg and everything else were suddenly going to sleep. Then the field locked in, and he saw everything through a haze of red cellophane. This field would enable them to survive the short run at hyperdrive.

There was a second's pause, and then the *Dark Star* vanished from the region of the unstable world, thrown away at incredible speed to a precalculated point in free space—a point far removed from the debris of a shattered planet to come.

Behind them, the bomb, quiet and alone now, continued down toward the planet's surface.

Though the force field fogged his vision, Talby could still see the stars. Only now they were rushing to greet him—all sizes and all degrees of magnitude, rushing toward him. But the distorting blur of hyperdrive allowed him to greet only a few in return. They fell at him like horizontal rain, pelting him with color as they rushed past and disappeared.

Supposedly it wasn't safe for a man to stay up in the observation dome while the ship was in hyperdrive. The shielding provided by the transparent hemisphere was minimal, and it was theorized that in hyperdrive a person might be subjected to a dangerously concentrated burst of radiation.

Talby, however, had disproved this particular theory, as he had disproved so many others. He'd survived eighteen such flights now, and his body was as healthy as ever. Healthier than that of anyone else on board, which, considering that he spent no time in the exercise room, Doolittle was at a loss to explain.

Talbly told him it was due to peace of mind, but Doolittle insisted there had to be something more than that. Perhaps the hypothesizers were right, but wrong. Perhaps anyone who remained in the dome during hyperdrive did receive a concentrated dose of radiation. Radiation that was not dangerous, but benign. Radiation that supplied something special to a man. Because there was no denying that Talby defied a large number of accepted rules for interstellar travel and came out of it in peculiarly good shape.

No one saw the bomb reach its predetermined detonation point just above the planet's surface. They were already too far away for that. But behind them, a blinding ball of white light appeared where the unstable world had once drifted. It turned pink, then crimson—a monstrous, blood-colored blossom blooming in uncaring night.

Then it faded rapidly and was gone. A world had vanished from the galaxy. Its convulsive death had given life to several new clusters of asteroids and meteors. These would now take their place among the other cosmic debris roaming the starpaths.

The universe came to an abrupt halt. The *Dark Star* stopped, its hyperdrive sequence concluded.

The red haze of the field faded from his eyes, drawn back into its electronic cage. Talby blinked.

He made a quick check of his instruments. They were safely out of hyperdrive. All navigational equipment was functioning properly, and they were on course. His hand moved toward the intercom switch. He intended to relay this information to Doolittle but, as so often happened, something more important caught his eye, dragged him away from human concerns.

Just to the lower right of their present course lay a particularly handsome purple and red nebula. They would pass quite close to it if they continued on their present path. He should have ample time to enjoy and study the new miracle.

His hand continued to hover halfway between the intercom activator and the arm of his chair-lounge. Then he relaxed in the seat. As astronomer it was still his job to make manual verification of the bomb run. But suppose he didn't? Suppose he didn't, and the bomb had malfunctioned? The scenario was simple to imagine. The world in the system they had just left would be explored and settled. Eventually it might grow to support a population larger than Earth's.

Then, one distant day, a planet thought safe would go spinning off its orbit into the sun, perhaps turning it in a few days into a churning nova which would sear the settled world clean of billions of lives. And no one could do more than rant and curse at the long-dead Talby. He would have returned a blow for the natural, unmanipulated universe. But he couldn't do it.

After all, they'd blame the entire crew of the *Dark Star*, and Talby couldn't drag the others down to an ignominious future no matter what he saw as fit for himself.

So he swung about in the chair, touched several buttons, and prepared to do his duty—for Doolittle, Pinback, Boiler, and Powell, and not for some faraway abstracted humanity.

The eyepiece to the deep-space telescope dipped neatly down in front of him. He edged close to it, and took a visual sighting. A rapidly diminishing bright spot was all that showed in the now considerable distance. Quick cross-check of charts revealed it was indeed something in the vicinity of the star they had just left. He addressed the intercom.

"Lieutenant Doolittle, it just exploded. Ah, the planet just exploded, sir. Lieutenant?"

Well, if Doolittle didn't even *care*. . . . Talby flipped the intercom off, morosely contemplated the heavens.

But it wasn't Doolittle's fault. The intercom, like so many things on the *Dark Star* lately, was merely malfunctioning again.

Down in the control room, with the bomb run no doubt successful and the destruction sequence completed, Pinback, Doolittle, and Boiler were taking a stretch, shifting about in their seats like so many old cats.

"Computer's late again," observed Boiler. "That computer's beginning to worry me, Doolittle. Sometimes I think I hear it singing to itself."

"I know it's late, Boiler," the lieutenant replied. "Don't let that bother you. It's about the only instrument on this ship that's still performing up to par." There was a cessation of the muted hum that always came over the speakers, and Doolittle smiled slightly. "See, there it is now."

"Attention, attention," the mechanical, mildly feminine machine voice said. "Ship's computer to all personnel. The hyperdrive sequence is now terminated, and I am happy to report that the target planet is destroyed."

"Whoopee," muttered Boiler, making a little circle in the air with one finger.

"You may now relax and take a stretch if you so desire, gentlemen."

"Unlock fail-safe," ordered Doolittle, ignoring the voice. It didn't do to listen too long to those mildly erotic tones.

Pinback was doing something at an overhead panel. "Fail-safe unlocked."

"The sector just visited," the computer continued, "is now cleared for colonization. You have successfully eliminated the only unstable world in the system. Congratulations on another successful bomb run, boys."

"Gosharootie, thanks, computer," Doolittle said sardonically. "Tell me, honey, what are you doing after the cataclysm tonight?"

"Operating the ship, as usual, Lieutenant Doolittle." There was a pause, then the voice continued in a slightly reproving fashion, "I must remind you again, Lieutenant, that these mental conceptualizations you have of me as a smooth-skinned, pliant, and heavy-breathing female humanoid are neither healthy nor conducive to the smooth operation of the ship. I must ask you to discontinue them."

"Oh, go discontinue yourself," Doolittle blurted curtly. "Stop panting, Pinback . . . you're fogging up your instruments." Pinback looked abashed and started to pout again.

The computer didn't reply to Doolittle's advice, recognizing either the frustration in the lieutenant's voice or else the impossibility of complying with the suggestion —or maybe both.

The thought left a sour taste in Doolittle's mind. He always got like this when a bomb run had been completed and they were faced once more with long days of nothing to do. Post-coital letdown, he thought disgustedly.

Irritated, nervous—he felt they had to hurry and find another system with habitable worlds and an unstable companion. And it was getting worse. The glow of satisfaction, the smooth aura of accomplishment that usually came over him after a successful run had grown shorter and shorter with each successive drop. Now it was practically nonexistent. He could remember when the pleasure of seeing an unstable world dissolved to its component elements had left him feeling good for weeks.

Now, he was empty again.

"What now, Boiler?" he found himself asking. "What have you got for us now?"

"So soon, Lieutenant?" wondered Pinback. "We only just finished a run." Doolittle ignored the sergeant.

Boiler, quiet and responsive to Doolittle's moods, was already hard at work with the predictors. "Not much here, Lieutenant. I don't see any possibilities at all in this sector. Tough."

Responsive, yes, but insensitive. Damn the man's insensitivity. Damn his uncommunicativeness and his inability to enjoy extended, intelligent conversation. Doolittle wondered at himself. He never would figure out why he preferred talking to Boiler instead of Pinback. Maybe it was because the corporal, at least, required nothing of him in return. Doolittle had never been a person to give much of himself. He expected too much from Boiler, and got too much from Pinback. If only Talby were more willing to chat. If only Powell were still around, to give the orders.

"Well, find me something," he ordered nervously. "I don't care where it is. Something interesting, anything . . . we've only got one lousy bomb left and then we can . . . go home—I think."

"Something interesting," Boiler echoed. "Okay." He bent to his instrumentation, consulted the charts from under his panel.

"Well, we're close to the Horsehead Nebula sector. We had reports before we left that there was as much as a ninety-five-percent probability of intelligent life in the southern quadrant of the nebula. Long-distance locators found at least two sol-type stars there showing measure perturbations in their paths, indicative of planets at distances which would place them in the so-called life zones."

"Don't give me that kind of bull," Doolittle complained. "Intelligent life my ass! You oughta know by now, Boiler, that there's no intelligent life in this universe. None at all."

Including ourselves, of course, he added to himself. But this was no revelation. They had known that for

years, when prediction after prediction had failed to be
borne out. They'd visited and mapped dozens of worlds
where life should have sprung up independently and
flowered, and they'd found nothing but lower forms of
plants and animals, the highest being Pinback's pet
amorph, which they'd called the Beachball. A poor response to all their desperate hopes of finding intelligent
life.

No, they were alone—alone in a mocking infinity.
Only Talby seemed not to be alone.

"I know it's a long shot," Boiler responded quietly,
"but . . . " He watched the lieutenant carefully, but
his guarded optimism had no effect on Doolittle.

"Damned wild goose chase is what it is," the lieutenant finally commented. He grinned a little. "Remember
when Commander Powell found that 'ninety-nine-plus'
probability of intelligent life in a little system on line
with the Magellanic Cloud and for a couple of minutes
we all thought he meant we were *going* there?"

The corporal shook his head. He didn't rememder. A
hand indicated a particular readout.

"But there is a possibility this time, according
to . . . " Doolittle ignored him, still reminiscing.

What a shame! What a sad memory! And what a colossal disappointment. It nearly broke Powell's heart.

"Remember what we found when we did get to that
world, Boiler? Remember? Was it a race of giant huma-
noids waiting to welcome us as members of a world-
spanning intergalactic civilization? Or a planet of quiet
thinkers waiting for a new, vigorous people like ourselves to unload all the secrets of the universe on? Or
even a race of intelligent insects? Or revolting giant
slugs?

"No . . . nothing to love, nothing to be friends with,
nothing to even raise to a conscious level. Nothing to
even hate decently. A joke, a damned mindless vegetable—that's what we found. A limp balloon." His voice
rose higher, and both Boiler and Pinback watched him
anxiously.

"Fourteen goddamned light-years for a vegetable that

goes squawk and lets out a stink if it's touched! Remember that?"

"All right, I remember, I remember," confessed Boiler, trying to calm his companion.

Doolittle was aware that he was once again perilously close to going over the edge. He dropped his voice, would have jammed his hands into his pockets if he hadn't been sitting down. He looked away from the others.

"So anyway, don't give me any of that 'intelligent life' stuff. Find me something I can blow up."

Once more an uneasy quiet reigned in the control room of the *Dark Star*. Each man returned to his station, which had the virtue of not yelling, not screaming, not scratching, and not fighting back.

They shot along in silence faster than man had ever traveled before, for the *Dark Star* was the first of its kind. There had been no experimental predecessor; the *Dark Star* was, in itself, an experimental ship. An experimental starship would have been prohibitively expensive, so it was combined with this first, vital mission, built with knowledge drawn from the unmanned deep-space probes.

And it had worked out well. Only minor, irritating little things continued to break down. The ship itself continued to operate *almost* flawlessly—like her crew.

A sudden series of beeps erupted from Pinback's station. He blinked, leaned forward. A key shut off the noise.

"Hey," he said after studying the instruments, his expression lighting up, "new star."

No one reacted. He looked at Boiler, then Doolittle. Maybe they hadn't heard him. "Hey, guess what," he repeated a bit louder, "I got a new star on the readout."

Doolittle had produced a well-worn deck of cards. He was playing solitaire. Doolittle was very good at solitaire. He didn't lose often because he cheated.

"What kind?" he asked without looking up.

Pinback checked the instruments again. "Red dwarf.

It's a complete unknown, sir, not even listed on the 'possibles' charts, from what I can see."

Doolittle put a black queen on a red king, then a black jack on the queen. "Any planets?"

"Around a red dwarf, sir? Even if there were any the chances of them being inhabi—"

"I asked you if it had any planets, Sergeant."

"Oh, all right." Pinback checked the readout again. His expression bulged. "Wow, yeah—it says eight probables here! How about that!"

"Any of 'em good?"

"Well," Pinback guessed, "it's kind of hard to tell at this distance, but there might be. Boy, wouldn't that be something? Around a red dwarf?"

"I mean, are any of 'em bad," Doolittle corrected, putting an ace up.

"Oh." Pinback sounded depressed, reluctantly checked his readouts again. "Naw, all stable."

Doolittle just grunted.

"I suppose that means we aren't going to map them out?" No reply. "Geez, Lieutenant, a red dwarf with eight possible planets—I mean, we at least ought to make an equatorial survey."

"Not our job," Doolittle said quietly.

"But couldn't we in this case make one teeny weeny little exception?"

"No." Black ten on red jack.

There was peace in the control room for a while, except for the gentle click-clacking of cards flicking down on the computation board. Pinback stared at Doolittle until he was quite certain that the lieutenant had nothing further to say on the subject of the strange new system.

"Ah," he said finally, "what are you gonna name it?"

Doolittle hesitated, spoke without looking up again. "What?"

"Ah, you know . . . that star," Pinback continued anxiously. "What are you gonna name it?"

"Who cares?" Doolittle responded irritably. "I'm busy, Pinback . . . don't bother me, huh?"

"But it's a whole new star, Lieutenant. With planets.

Eight of 'em. Only a handful of human beings ever got to name a tiny, insignificant thing like maybe a river or a mountain or a sea. A few luckier ones got to name features on the surface of the Moon and Mars and the other planets. You can name a whole star system, Lieutenant."

Doolittle spared him a quick glance. "Look, don't bother me, please, Pinback? I've almost got this game played out. Leave me alone, hmmm?"

"Commander Powell would name it," Pinback finished, with the ultimate argument. He folded his arms firmly.

"Commander Powell's dead," reminded Doolittle for the thousandth time, putting a deuce up on the ace.

"Well then . . ." Pinback suddenly beamed. "That's it—'Don't Bother Me.' We'll name it 'Don't Bother Me.'" He hunted hurriedly under his station for the small semi-official log he'd been keeping ever since Doolittle had lost interest in making regular entries in the ship's printed log.

The pencil that was clipped to it was worn to a stub now, and he had to strain to write neatly with it.

"There," he said after an hour's dedicated scribbling. "All nice and official, with coordinates and everything. 'Don't Bother Me' . . . eight planets." He finished with a flourish. "Congratulations, Lieutenant."

Doolittle started to shout again, but he turned up the last card he needed to play out and was feeling instantly generous. After all, why pick on poor Pinback just because he was a mite overzealous in his job?

"Thanks, Sergeant. If any intelligent beings do live there, maybe they'll thank you someday. I know I wouldn't want myself to be visited by anything like me."

"Uh, Lieutenant," Pinback replied, his face twisted in uncertainty, "I'm not sure I know what you mean by—"

Boiler's deep tones broke in over him. "Hey, Doolittle, I got a goodie. Definitely unstable. Eighty-five-percent probability of an unstable planet in star system P-one-thirty-eight. Indication of habitable planets in same system: ninety-six percent. Chances are it will go off its orbit inside the critical period and hit its star." He looked up from his readouts. "Wanna blow it up?"

He laughed.

Pinback eyed him uneasily. Boiler didn't laugh very often, and Pinback could have done without even those occasional displays of humor on the corporal's part. But the information appeared to please Doolittle. He smiled broadly.

"Real good, Boiler. Real good work. That's what I'm looking for. Chart a course as fast as you can." His mind was singing, one more planet, one more bomb—and then they could go home, go home, go home . . . back to warm, comfortable, feeling Earth, back to real grass and real booze and members of the opposite sex. Back to the other aliens, back where they belonged . . .

Boiler was working feverishly at his console. "Hey, throw me the chart log, Pinback."

"Name it, then blow it up. Name it, then blow it up —that's all you guys ever wanna do," grumbled Pinback. But he reached beneath his seat, brought out the thick-bound volume of star charts, and tossed it into Boiler's lap.

Boiler glowered at him and just held the book for a second. Conscious of the suddenly charged atmosphere in the tiny control room, Doolittle watched the two men. Even Pinback, he realized, could be pushed past a certain critical point.

Boiler held his stare for a moment longer, then opened the book and started thumbing through pages. Doolittle relaxed. What Pinback might do if pushed beyond that certain hypothetical region was anybody's guess. Probably go stand in a corner and cry. But you never knew. Sometimes he suspected that Sergeant Pinback had unplumbed depths. Doolittle spent as much time keeping him and Boiler apart as he did running the ship.

There had never been as much trouble between the two when Commander Powell was alive. But that was all in the past. So much was all in the past, had been lost

in Powell's death. You remove one corner of the penta-
gram, and the mystic symbol seemed to lose all of its
power.

"Let's have some music in here, Boiler," he said carefully.

"Sure thing." Boiler, showing no signs of recent ag-
gravation, reached for an upper panel. Strains of the
song "Benson, Arizona" immediatly floated through the
control room.

Doolittle relaxed. He loved this particular tune almost
as much as he hated it. Loved it for the memories it
brought back to him, and hated it for reminding him of
what he no longer had.

Pinback spoke up a moment later—his usual obnoxious and cheerful self again. It didn't take Pinback long
to break out of one of his pouts. He was incapable, it
seemed to Doolittle, of getting really angry at anything.

"Hey, don't you think it's time to make an entry in
the log, Lieutenant? You know, bring the records up to
date, record officially the new star, tell about our little
amusing troubles, and all that."

Doolittle turned over three cards, found himself stuck
with the last jack buried on the bottom. He switched
the jack with the top card, then put it up on the queen
and played out the last two cards and the rest of the
game. That made 342 straight games he'd played out—
an impressive string he had no intention of breaking.

"What, Pinback?"

"I said, don't you think it's time for a log entry?"
When Doolittle didn't exactly leap to his feet to race to
the recorder, Pinback continued pleading. "Aw, come
on, Lieutenant. You haven't made a log entry in a long
time. One of these days that log'll be history. Little kids
will study it and gasp, and their great-grandparents will
say, 'I remember when the *Dark Star* first did this or
that.' The folks back home will—"

"The folks back home," Doolittle started to say angrily, "won't give a flying . . . !"

He stopped. It was impossible to get mad at Pinback.
The sergeant was a terrible audience. He wouldn't do

the decent thing and howl back at you. No, Pinback would either retreat into a heady pout or else try to make a joke out of your most heartfelt furies.

He could lay it on Boiler, but Boiler would just sit there and ignore him completely. At least Pinback reacted. And Talby, he could talk and yell and complain to Talby, but something in him always rejected the thought of disturbing the astronomer's period of endless contemplation.

He could always talk to Commander Powell. Even though Powell was technically deceased, his occasionally functioning mind was still capable of random conversation. Sometimes Doolittle found himself closer in feeling to Powell than anyone else. Both men's minds existed in a kind of suspended animation.

Well, might as well make Pinback happy. And it was part of his duty. And he'd promised himself, once upon a time, that he'd carry out the duties of acting commander to the best of his ability, etc., etc., blah-blah.

Besides, if he didn't do it, Pinback might, and that would be disastrous if they ever did get back in one piece.

He reached up and activated the overhead screen. When the READY sign had cleared, he spoke toward the directional microphone. "Ship's Log, entry number one thousand nine hundred and forty-three. Lieutenant Doolittle, acting commander of *Dark Star*, informing.

"Ship is presently cruising through sector Theta nine ninety at light-speed multiple enroute to area Veil Nebula for destruction of unstable planet. Our ETA is seventeen hours. Our ability to locate unstable worlds in systems with habitable planets seems to have increased markedly with practice. It almost seems as if they are presenting themselves to us on request. I can only assume that our increased proficiency is due to greater vigilance and familiarity with the necessary instrumentation. In any case it appears that we shall be returning home sooner than expected, ah, and we . . ."

He hesitated. There was something else, he thought, but he couldn't think of what . . . oh yes. "Ship's internal systems continue to deteriorate. We are compensating, but as the number of malfunctions multiplies, we find it increasingly difficult to improvise from our rapidly decreasing ship's stores."

Pinback leaned over and whispered to him.

He nodded, spoke to the screen. "Oh yeah . . . the short circuit in the rear seat panel which killed Commander Powell is still faulty. After much deliberation and thorough analysis of the situation, I have given explicit instructions that no one is to sit in that seat or he will be severely reprimanded."

Pinback leaned over and whispered again, a mite more urgently this time.

"The storage . . . what is it now, Pinback?"

He paused, listened to the whisper. "Oh. And because he is sitting next to Commander Powell's seat, Pinback is continually bothered by the faulty circuit. He is possessed of this unreasonable fear that his rear seat panel will be the next to short circuit.

I've pointed out to Sergeant Pinback that this attitude is both irrational and asinine, and he—"

"Is not," muttered Pinback from off-screen.

"—he persists in reminding me of it." Then the thought he had first been hunting for finally came to him. "Oh, yeah. Storage Area Nine, Subsection B self-destructed last week following a circuit malfunction, thus destroying the ship's entire supply of toilet paper. I would request of the folks down at McMurdo that we be immediately resupplied with this important commodity. But am afraid, logistics being what they seem to be at Earth Base these days, that they would ship us the toilet paper in lieu of our desperately needed radiation shielding.

"As the two materials are not interchangeable in function, I am threfore delaying the request that we be resupplied with the former commodity, although," and he looked over at Pinback, "there are those among the crew who feel that in the long run, the toilet paper is the more vitally needed of the two."

He stared back up into the screen. "And if anyone

ever reading this log finds the present situation amusing, I can only hope that they someday find themselves in a situation where they have to opt for radiation shielding over toilet paper. I think that's all."

He reached up and switched off the screen recorder, feeling pleased with himself. It was a good log entry, a substantial log entry. It would never get him promoted, of course, but it was sobering to think that someday what he had just recorded might be broadcast to reverent billions all over Earth.

The music was beginning to grate in its familiarity, both of sound and conjured-up image. He swiveled around to glance at the silent corporal. "Put something else on, Boiler. Something less descriptive. Something more . . . abstract."

Boiler mumbled something unintelligible, nudged the dial a fraction. Immediately, responsive electric guitars, drums, trumpets, and theremin filled the tiny control cabin, swamped it in an orgy of amplified rhythm.

Pinback and Boiler began to move in their seats, drawn together by their single, common point of interest —jumping, rocking, snapping their fingers, shaking in time to the music.

Doolittle tried to join them, to complete the triumvirate. He tried to force himself, but for all his will to subsume himself in the music, all that moved was his head, slightly. Inside, he wondered that he could respond to the music at all.

Something made him different from even Boiler and Pinback. Yet again, he wondered what it was that he was missing.

The music reached Talby over the open intercom. He frowned slightly until he identified the source of the interruption and turned it down. It would be unprofessional as well as potentially dangerous to switch the intercom off entirely. He hardly heard the music anyway.

That music.

2

THEY CONTINUED ON that way through space—the *Dark Star*'s drive engines eating up the light-years, each man occupied in his own thoughts. So no one monitored the detection instruments, no one saw the thing appear.

Talby was intent on the stars behind them, and his three fellow crewmembers concentrated on the music inside them. So they didn't see the initially faint, still incredibly distant luminosity that had appeared in the path of the ship. Didn't see the twister of free energy that danced and leaped and frolicked among a million-kilometer-long cluster of uneven fragments. Fragments of a long-dead world in a long-forgotten system, perhaps even a system set in a galaxy other than this one.

Some of these fragments carried a strong negative charge, others positive. Some were neutral, and some possessed electrical properties that would have driven an energy engineer to hysterics. Gigantic discharges of brilliantly colored energy played about the millions of solid components that formed the vortex.

It was the sixth member of the *Dark Star*'s crew, the one immune both to astrophysical daydreaming and to electric rock mesmerism, who finally noticed the rapidly approaching threat. And it was this sixth member who cut off the music to the control room.

Pinback, Boiler, and Doolittle slowed, stopped their in-place dancing. At first Doolittle thought that it was just another of the seemingly endless series of mechanical malfunctions. A soft female voice corrected him moments later.

"Attention, attention, ship's computer calling all personnel. I have been required to disengage your recreational music. Repeat. Ship's computer to all personnel, this is an emergency override. All systems must stand by for emergency directive. Information for procedure will follow."

"What the hell?" muttered Doolittle.

Pinback looked over at him wide-eyed, questioning. Boiler just sat and muttered. "Better be something damned important to break into my music."

"Extrasolar concatenation of solid matter of uncertain properties is approaching at point nine-five light-speed on collision course. Predictions indicate that the body of matter is fairly dense, yet still spread too widely for us to avoid it without risking permanent structural damage to all noninorganic personnel on board."

"Why can't you call it an asteroid storm like I asked you to?" Doolittle complained.

"For the same reason," the computer voice shot back, a little peevishly, "that I cannot refer to you as Grand Admiral Doolittle of His Majesty's Terran Imperial Fleet Forces, Lieutenant. Both are nonscientific, inaccurate, imaginary references concocted by you while acting under the influence of juvenile literary material and—"

"Call it an asteroid storm," Doolittle warned, having totally forgotten that something important was about to happen, "or I'll see your primary circuit disconnected."

"You cannot do that, Lieutenant," said Pinback, shocked.

"You cannot do that, Lieutenant," confirmed the computer. "My primary circuit cannot be disengaged while outside of Earth Base's broadcast influence, and only under the direct supervision of . . ." There was a pause while hidden instruments monitored the lieutenant's internal configuration of the moment.

"However, I will take your current mental state into account. The . . . *asteroid storm* . . ."

"That's better," grinned a satisfied Doolittle.

". . . is approaching the ship on collision course."

"Doesn't mean a thing," Doolittle said smugly to the others. "We'll slip through even the densest storm without meeting anything bigger than a pebble, and our deflectors will handle any oddball-sized chunks."

"Very true, Lieutenant," the computer continued dryly. "However, *this* particular storm appears to be bound together by an electromagnetic energy vortex like the one we ran into two years ago. Is that sufficiently descriptive, Lieutenant Doolittle?"

But Doolittle had become momentarily speechless with shock, as had Pinback and Boiler. All remembered that first encounter, and what it had almost done to them.

"I see that it is," the computer went on. "Normally I wouldn't bother you boys with this problem, but as you recall, my defensive circuits controlling our prime external force screens were destroyed in that other storm. Therefore, you now have left approximately thirty—"

"Move," some voice was screaming inside Doolittle, "move, move," but he was frozen helpless in his seat, unable to reach for a single control, unable even to question the computer.

"— -five seconds left in which to manually activate all defensive systems. I would urge some speed at this point, gentlemen, as you now have only . . ."

Time, or rather the lack of it, finally shocked Doolittle into action. Pinback and Boiler came out of stasis a split second later.

"Lock gravity systems!" an urgent, nervous voice—his—was saying.

"Artificial gravity locked," came Pinback's efficient response. The three men were extensions of the ship now, each working at maximum capability.

"Activate HR-three," Doolittle continued.

"Activated." This from Boiler, as he smoothly checked gauges and adjusted controls.

"Lock air pressure."

"Air-pressure lock activated," responded Pinback.

"Four. All systems activated. All screens powered up," Doolittle told them.

"Roger . . . count four," agreed Pinback.

"Lock all defensive systems," finished Doolittle. "And pray," he added under his breath. He'd have to hope Boiler and Pinback picked up on that thought by themselves—he had no time to lead them in a formal service.

Another duty he had somehow lost track of over the months, years. He was also supposed to serve as ship's minister. Maybe he could get Talby to take that over . . .

The *Dark Star* took on a pale red aura as the defensive screens came up to full readiness.

"Defensive systems locked in!" Pinback shouted as the chronometer ticked off the last seconds. Doolittle took a second to admire him. The sergeant would make a good officer some day if . . . if . . .

It seemed to Doolittle that there was some important, critical reason why Pinback would never be able to make a good officer someday, and it had nothing to do with his ability. It was something else, something more basic. It escaped him at the moment, but . . .

"Lock final force field," he instructed the others.

Again he felt the familiar tingle, the sensation of having his whole body fall lightly asleep, as the internal force field took hold. Not to protect them this time from a jump through hyperspace, but from any damage the storm might inflict.

Of course, if it was as severe as the last one of its kind they had ridden out, there was always the chance that the ship wouldn't survive in one piece. In that case the three men would remain in-field until the generating machinery broke down or was destroyed. If the machinery and engines remained intact, they would stay in the force field forever, unable to move, slowly aging away, helpless to repair the damaged circuitry.

The vortex was on the screen now, visible to the naked eye. It looked bigger than the first one Doolittle remembered. A writhing, spinning mass of energy, leaping from particle to solid particle in gigantic discharges.

Of the solid material itself nothing could be seen at such a distance. Instrumentation revealed it to be a typical mixture, from microscopic dust to occasional chunks larger than the *Dark Star* itself. Now and then one of the larger pieces of cosmic debris came close enough to impact on the ship's defensive screens and was gently jostled aside.

The danger was from the billions of volts of free energy playing haphazardly in free space, not from any loose hunk of rock, however impressive it might look on the screens. Doolittle winced every time the field light over the screen flared, indicating that the defensive screens were drawing energy.

Not everyone viewed the approaching storm with alarm. Up in the observation dome, Talby was ecstatic. The iridescent holocaust was overwhelmingly beautiful. The dazzling discharges of energy exploded across his field of vision in complex patterns of their own, only slightly distorted by the protective shielding of dome.

He'd swung his observation chair 180 degrees so that the storm was pouring directly at him and past. Everything seemed to be happening in slow motion—an effect of the force field, which concurrent with protecting them also dropped body function time to the minimum necessary to support life.

In normal time the eruptions of color would have flowed past in a blur of unrecognizable shapes. But in the slowed-down universe of the force field, the colossal bolts took on definite shape and form, reduced them to visions his dazed mind could comprehend.

Magnificent, glorious, incomparable—the astronomer was drunk on the beauty. That it might at any moment shred the ship and himself like foil bothered him not a whit.

The load on the screens was tremendous, but they held . . . held while the storm passed over and around the enveloped *Dark Star*, held till it was safely past—almost.

A huge chunk of charged material drifted close in the rear of the storm. The *Dark Star* was the nearest body of comparable mass, and the bolt that leaped the distance between matter and ship was of truly prodigious size.

It penetrated the force screen and struck the ship lightly, almost caressingly, at the lowest point of the craft, just below the emergency airlock. Although the untiring screens still absorbed most of the blow, events followed which were not normal.

A tiny, insignificant portion of the energy that had impacted on the ship traveled through the outer, then inner walls, and reached a particular circuit. A particularly vital circuit. Several internal fluid-state controls were activated, and a sign appeared unexpectedly on the main screen in the computer room:

BOMB BAY SYSTEMS ACTIVATED

As the last of the storm passed the ship, the huge doors in its belly separated and a rectangular object moved smoothly downward. A large number 20 was inscribed on its side.

Within the computer itself, cross-references were rapidly checked, the cause of the malfunction traced, and results, if any, compared. The conclusion that something had happened which shouldn't have was quickly reached.

"Computer to bomb number twenty," the computer said, using human speech since it was impossible for numbers to be misinterpreted in verbal form. "Return to the bomb bay immediately." The last solid particles, final residue of the storm, bounced off the still-activated force field, extended now to encompass the bomb as well as the ship.

There was a pause, then the bomb objected mildly, "But I have received the operational signal. It came through normal channels and was processed accordingly."

Not expecting an argument, the central computer hesitated briefly. It finally decided on direct contradiction as the most effective—and safest—method of remonstration.

"The signal was given due to a temporary malfunction in the activating mechanism. This is not a bomb run. Cancel all drop programming immediately." The computer tried to inject a note of insistence into its voice.

"Nevertheless, I've received the signal to prepare for a drop and shall continue . . ."

"Emergency override," came the ultimate command from the computer. "Return to the bay."

"Very well, then," bomb number twenty responded. It slid obediently back up on its shaft. The bay doors closed beneath it. As they did so the last vestiges of the storm receded into the distance.

The force field lapsed, and Talby turned quickly to watch the mass of flickering color and ceaseless energy retreat, heading for uncharted reaches. He waved it a mental goodbye. After all, danger or no, the storm seemed very much alive. Maybe it was a strange kind of organism, contained within itself, forever unable to make safe contact with another creature except one of its own kind.

Ah, there you go, anthropomorphizing again, Talby. He chastised himself. The storm was a manifestation of purely physical phenomena, he instructed himself firmly. Nothing more nor less. He turned and resumed his quiet study of the fore starfield.

The force field and the ship's defensive screens automatically shut down with the passing of the danger. Doolittle, Pinback, and Boiler slumped heavily in their seats, letting the tension flow out of them.

Pinback forced a slight grin as he removed his headset. "Well, we made it again."

"Yeah," agreed Doolittle. "I wonder why we did. There was enough power in that vortex to melt this tin triangle to slag. I didn't think anything on it worked that well anymore." He noticed a red light winking steadily on his console.

"And maybe it doesn't." At Pinback's curious glance, he nodded toward the indicator."

"Now what?" Then, louder, "Go ahead, computer. We're out of stasis and recovered."

"Attention, attention," the computer began, ignoring the fact that Doolittle and Pinback were already hanging on every coming word. "Ship's computer to bridge. There was a malfunction aboard ship during the final passage of the concatenation of . . . during the final passage of the asteroid storm."

Pinback and Doolittle exchanged tired glances. It couldn't be very serious or the operation of the ship would have been noticeably affected by now. Doolittle groaned.

"All right, computer . . . what is it?"

"Tracing."

While Doolittle waited irritably—they would never get their music back on until the damned machine had finished its report—smoke drifted from a small hole in the wall of the emergency airlock.

Needless to say, neither the hole nor the drifting smoke was a normal component of the silent airlock. It drifted out from behind a panel that covered a small chamber. Within that chamber rested an operating laser that occasionally now flashed in a sequence not programmed for it. It was an especially important laser. It was the center of the malfunction. But the reason the computer couldn't locate it was because that last, parting bolt from the storm had burned out its connections with the computer.

"I have not yet identified the nature of the problem," was all the machine voice said to Doolittle. "Shall I contact you when I find out what this malfunction is?"

"Yeah," put in the heretofore silent Boiler. "Do that . . . but meantime, shut up, huh?" The computer didn't reply, but became silent.

Boiler was up, unstrapping himself from his seat. Doolittle was ahead of him, and Pinback hurrying to catch up.

"I don't know about the rest of you, but I need to

look at something besides these damned controls for a while. Let's get out of here."

"I could use a rest, too," added Boiler. "Good thing we weren't resting when that storm hit." They were leaving the control room now, heading down the corridor leading back toward one of the converted storage rooms—the one they'd converted for their own use.

Boiler was in an unusually talkative mood. "I remember the last time we were in an asteroid storm. I was down in the 'A' food locker getting a sandwich when I heard the damn sleeping quarters blow out."

"Yeah, me too," chirped Pinback. "Boy, you wouldn't think just a little escaping air could make such a racket!" Doolittle gave him a tired look but the sergeant continued on enthusiastically.

"Say, you know, you guys," he began as they turned a bend in the corridor, "if we really wanted to, really decided to put in a little work, we could fix up the sleeping quarters like they were before. Then we could sleep on real pneumatic bunks again. Hey, guys," he said pleadingly, "why don't we fix up the sleeping quarters so we can have a decent place to sleep again? Huh? Why don't we? It wouldn't be too hard.

"All we'd have to do is patch up the hole in the ship and pump some air back in. We could even do most of it from inside, I bet. Hey, guys . . ."

"Shut up, Pinback," Doolittle muttered. Then the thought that had been bothering him clicked and he glanced back at Boiler.

"What do you mean you were getting a sandwich? There's not supposed to be any real food on this ship. All we're supposed to have on board are these nutritious and wholesome concentrates. Not any real food. You couldn't make a sandwich out of concentrates. Where'd you get the stuff?"

Boiler looked slightly apologetic as they approached the door marked FOOD LOCKER NO. 2. Even a mite embarrassed. His voice was unnaturally defensive.

"Well, you remember that each of us was allowed four crates of personal stuff for the trip?"

"Yeah, so?" pressed Doolittle.

Boiler hesitated slightly, then asked, "You remember the too marked *Books*? They were supposed to be full of astrophysics manuals and good stuff I was to study and comment on while we were traveling?"

Doolittle nodded; he was beginning to make connections. It was just that he'd never suspect Boiler—plain, unimaginative, stolid Boiler—of such daring duplicity. Evidentally, neither had the inspectors who had passed the crates.

"The night before we transferred from Earth Orbital Station to the ship," the corporal continued, "I threw 'em all out the station disposal lock."

"So the two crates were full of bread," guessed Doolittle, "and what else?"

"Bread," Boiler nodded in a mournful way it was sad to see, "and peanut butter and jelly . . . all kinds of jelly. Also swiss cheese, kosher salami, sardines, mayonnaise, pickle relish, corned beef, pastrami, lettuce, and knockwurst." He shook his head. "I really miss that knockwurst."

"And you were holding out on us," accused Doolittle softly, "while we were masticating that colored crap concentrate? You were eating salami, and corned beef, and . . . and . . ." he tried to say pastrami, but his mouth was so full of saliva at the thought that he couldn't.

"You could have done the same thing," Boiler protested, drawing himself up with a modicum of dignity. "Anyhow, I'd just about broken down and decided to share it with you guys when the first storm hit.

"Most of our personal stuff was up in the room with the rest of our things. It was insulated pretty good. I used to sneak it out and take it down to the food locker to eat because it was the only place I could get rid of the scraps and not have to worry about the odors." His expression grew even sadder.

"When the sleeping quarters went, so did the crate full of real food. I just hope if there *is* any intelligent life out there, that they find that floating mass of gunk first. Then they'll know we're civilized."

There was a moment of silence, in memorium. Doolittle said a silent prayer for the now-space-petrified pastrami and looked at Boiler with new respect. The shock he had been concealing must have been terrible.

"I'm sorry, Boiler. I really am."

"Ah, that's all right, Lieutenant. I've pretty much gotten over it. I'm only sorry I didn't get to share it with you guys after all.

"That shouldn't keep us from fixing up the sleeping quarters again," put in Pinback, whose tone showed no feeling for Boiler's state of mind. He opened the door and preceded them into the converted food locker.

Pinback's urgent desire to repair the formal sleeping quarters took on added weight with the actual sight of their present abode. Three highly unpneumatic bunks lay scattered against the thick walls. They were emergency-grade only, and a far cry from the zero-gee sleeping cots of pre-explosion days.

Assorted debris of the kind commonly cast off by the bachelor human male covered bunks and floor and walls with fine impartiality—a liberal coating of useless flotsam composed of worn-out objects of every conceivable shape and former function.

Only one bunk lay neat and spotless. The blanket across it was drawn taut enough to bounce a coin on. Dress insignia and medals were laid out across it in order preparatory to donning.

It was Talby's bunk, of course. Talby's bunk, which hadn't been used in . . . Doolittle couldn't remember how long. Couldn't remember when the astronomer had begun sleeping in his observation chair up in the dome. He didn't like it, but nothing in the regulations said any member of the crew couldn't sleep wherever he wished.

But Doolittle didn't think it was healthy.

Three of the walls were bare, the locker shelving having been completely removed when the men decided to move in. The fourth wall was covered from ceiling to floor with glossy color photos of female-type humans.

There were several hundred photos, blown up from microfilm. Some of them were intact, others were cut to show off some particular portion of the subject's anatomy. They had one thing in common, and that was that artificial clothing figured in none of them.

"It wouldn't take but a day or two to fix it up, Doolittle, Boiler. Aw, c'mon, fellas. We could do it in—"

"Shut up, Pinback," Doolittle yelled.

"Oh, have it your own way, then. Sleep on a lumpy bunk—see if I care." Pinback flopped down on his own mattress. Quick fumbling at his own supplies produced a cigarette.

Doolittle relaxed on his bunk and produced a packet of cards, began laying them out for yet another game of solitaire. Boiler sat down on his bed and stared at one of the blank walls.

"For your enjoyment," came the soothing voice of the computer, which in addition to running the ship constantly monitored what it believed to be their needs, "we now present some moonlight melodies of Martin Segundo and his Scintilla Strings.

"Our first selection is the perennial favorite, 'When Twilight Falls on NGC Eight Nine One'." Soft music filled the untidy alcove. No one bothered to object. The computer's arguments about the importance of mood music as opposed to violent rock could be maddening. Only when its choices grew extremely puerile did they bother to fight it.

Boiler had shuffled about in his own locker, came up with a fat cigar. The computer voice drifted in over the music.

"I must remind both Corporal Boiler and Sergeant Pinback that more than one person smoking at a time puts an unwholesome strain upon the air-purification system."

"What air-purification system?" Boiler snorted derisively. "I can still smell last week's smoke." The computer didn't deign to reply.

Boiler lit up disdainfully, began blowing extremely neat smoke rings. At times the presence of full artificial gravity on the *Dark Star* was to be regretted. Sleeping hours were among them, especially since their special bunks had been ruined. Now was another of them, as Boiler contemplated his nebula-like creations and considered the possible reactions of smoke rings in zero-gee.

Pinback was staring at the picture-covered wall, the cigarette still grasped unlit in one hand, the virgin match in the other. Abruptly he let them both drop to the floor. His face took on a decidedly sly expression.

There was a lively gleam in his eyes as he picked up a large box and set it on his bed. Watching Boiler and Doolittle for signs of reaction, he began fumbling through its contents. Boiler blew contented smoke rings.

The corporal rolled over, selected another cigar, and lit it. He seemed surprised to discover then that he had another already in his mouth. Without seeming the least bit embarrassed, he put out the second one by pinching the tip into suffocation.

A moment later he had exchanged it for a switchblade knife—an odd item to bring on board, and one which the mission directors would have banned if they had known about it. But the one thing the psychometricians had insisted on was that every man's four crates of personal effects, barring actual explosives or something equally dangerous, were absolutely private.

This was why Boiler had had such success in bringing along such unorthodox but decidedly nonexplosive items as his real-sandwich components and the switchblade. The latter snicked open with a wicked metallic whisper.

Holding the knife in one hand, he used the other to clear everything from the upturned crate alongside his bed. It made a nice makeshift table. This was one of his own, personal, surviving crates. It was made of good solid homey wood, not plastic or free-formed metal.

Spreading his fingers flat on the surface, he took the knife and began mumblety-pegging with it, jabbing between the closely spaced fingers into the firm wood. He started outside the thumb and worked over to the outside of the little finger. Then he repeated the journey.

Back and forth, forth and back, and back—and the knife sliced down just outside one of his fingers. He stopped, held up his nicked hand, and stared blankly at it.

All the attributes and faults that the psyche people had agreed were present in Boiler were apparent right then: that he had ice water in his veins; that he was likely to be the least communicative member of the *Dark Star* crew; that he would be the one least likely to crack in a pressure situation—except for Powell.

They had told him all that before they had left for Earth Orbital Station, at the final psyche briefing. He studied the finger, remembered what they had told him, and smiled.

Since he had only ice water in his veins, then of course there could be only ice water leaking out. And that would stop quickly enough. Indeed, while the knife had been driven into the finger with some force, anyone could see for himself that there was no blood dripping out. That this was due to Boiler's unnatural control of his own body was the explanation of the psychometricians who had first observed the quality in him.

Of course, the distinct possibility existed that he was imagining his own lack of bleeding, that he was in actuality spurting gore all over the room, and that he had better seek treatment quickly or else bleed to death. In which case he was mad.

His smile grew broader, then vanished. But he wasn't at all mad. Only Talby was mad, and he was harmless. Boiler wondered if Talby, mad Talby, would bleed.

One of these days, maybe he'd find out.

Pinback was having trouble concealing a smile of his own as he removed a strange object from the colorless box. It was a pair of eyeglasses of unusual properties. Possibly two people on Earth would have found it amusing. Despite this, somewhat more than two of these objects had been manufactured on that benighted planet. Pinback put on the glasses.

They consisted of a cheap plastic frame on which

were mounted a pair of grossly bloodshot half-eyeballs made of cheaper plastic and attached to the glasses by means of metal springs.

Bending his head and carefully concealing the device from view, he moved slowly toward Boiler. The corporal had concluded the extensive examination of his invulnerable finger and was now leaning against the wall and blowing his perfect smoke rings once more. Pinback slowly leaned over and toward him—ever so slowly. He knelt slightly and bent his head, removing his hand at just the right time, and the eyeballs flopped out of their frames to bob wildly on the springs.

Boiler turned with equal patience and calmly blew a fresh smoke ring into Pinback's waiting face. There was a moment of nonreaction. Then Pinback turned and made his way back to his own bunk, his smile gone. Dejectedly, he removed the glasses and dropped them back into the box.

Boiler's crazy, the poor slob, he thought. Cuts his own finger and doesn't say a thing. Crazy, but he won't let me help.

Boiler stared evenly at Pinback, then went back to introspective contemplation of his seemingly uninjured finger. Nuts, the sergeant was certifiably nuts! They were all nuts, except maybe Doolittle—and Doolittle had other problems.

The silence was getting to Pinback, as it always did. There must be something he could do for the poor guys. Something he could do . . . His gaze left the floor and settled on the nearby form of Doolittle.

The lieutenant was once again deep into a game of solitaire. Pinback's mouth started to curl mischievously at the corners. He started rummaging through the bottomless box.

Doolittle, meanwhile, had searched through the deck card by card until he had found a red jack to put on the vacant queen. He was oblivious to Pinback, to Boiler, to the room, and to the ship.

The voice inside his head was admonishing him again.

Most of the time he could shut it out, but sometimes it got so insistent that no wall could dampen it fully.

"You're cheating again, Doolittle," it claimed angrily, beating at him relentlessly. "You've always cheated, you know that, Doolittle?

"You cheated to get into flight school, and then you cheated on your astronaut physical when you couldn't pass the pull-ups. They said that was impossible, but you did it, Doolittle. You cheated on the oral exam when you wanted to get on the *Dark Star* mission to impress your girl friend, and you cheated with the psychiatrist, giving him all the carefully prepared right answers instead of the truthful ones.

"You cheated your way all the way through your short, miserable, successful life, Lieutenant Doolittle— and you're paying for it, in triplicate. Because right now"—he put a red ten on the jack—"right now you'd like to cheat yourself back home, wouldn't you?

"But you can't, because now there's nobody left to cheat here but yourself. If you go home without the computer confirming that you've properly utilized all twenty of those expensive little toys in the bomb bay, they'll turn you to powder. And if you try and dump the last one in no particular place, the computer will record it and they won't be complimentary when you get home, will they?

"No, Doolittle. They'll most likely toss you in the can for observation. Then they'll find out about your other cheating and despite all your successes they'll be *most* displeased. Your only out was to fool the computer, and you can't do that, can you? So it looks like you're stuck with doing a good job in spite of yourself, hey?

"You could never fool Commander Powell, either— but then, at least he understood."

He jerked sharply. Someone was standing next to him . . .

The moment of fright passed quickly, turned to anger. It wasn't the long-dead Powell. It was only Pinback. He went back to his game.

Pinback reached stealthily inside his flight suit, whipped out an object of uncertain shape, and dangled it jerkily in front of Doolittle's face. It was a rubber chicken. Doolittle was not impressed.

He put a black eight on a red eight: an impossibility to resolve, even for an accomplished cheater. Taking the rest of the cards, he threw them down on top of the pile.

"Damn it!" He glared briefly at Pinback, who recoiled under that momentary unaccustomed blast of intense hatred, and left the room.

He was furious at himself. Furious for putting the wrong card on the wrong card. Furious at Pinback and his idiotic rubber fowl. Furious at the universe that mocked him, and worse—ignored him.

A badly confused Pinback let the rubber chicken hang loosely at his side and looked dazedly over at Boiler.

"Now what do you suppose is the matter with him?"

He had to calm down, Doolittle told himself. Had to. The others were depending on him. He couldn't continue to fly off the handle at poor Pinback like that. Of course, the sergeant only invited it with his infantile attempts at humor, but Doolittle ought to be able to cope with that by now. Pinback wasn't responsible for his childish activities.

In fact, it seemed for a moment to Doolittle that Pinback wasn't even responsible for being on this mission. But that was a ridiculous thought!

Got to relax, got to take it easy, he instructed himself.

The music room. That was it, he'd go to the music room. He walked faster. It wasn't far.

3

HE SLID BACK to the door. The music room was a sub-
divided section of the common recreation chamber,
walled off for his own use. Closing the door behind him,
he turned and gazed reverently at the organ.

Using up almost all of their preformed wood scraps
and everything he could generate out of the glass-mak-
ing set, he'd made the instrument entirely by hand in the
ship's crafts-and-manual-hobby shop.

Out of what he could create from that, and from material cannibalized from several musical instruments
(provided by the thoughtful psychometricians), he had
produced something that resembled a cross between a
weaver's loom, an upright piano, and a spice vendor's
pushcart.

Dozens of bottles and bells and pieces of wood were
suspended from a high wooden rack-and-shelf arrangement. All were connected by a mad spiderweb of strings
and wires to a central keyboard.

Sitting gently in the chair, he took a mallet and tried
several bottles for sound. The first few were fine, but
eventually he struck one that gave back an inconsistent
hollow bong. That same damned half-liter jug. It would
never stay tuned.

A pitcher of water was standing to one side. Half of it

had evaporated since he had last played here. Had it been that long? Ah well, nothing was lost. The water was recycled constantly by the ship, from normal breathing, excretion, and standing jugs.

Taking up the mallet, he tapped the half-liter again, poured some water into it, tapped it. More water, another tap, and a last dram of liquid should make it just right.

Someday he would finish the organ and get it properly tuned. Someday. Tuning an organ was, after all, a considerable job. But now it was as ready as he could get it. He raised his hands dramatically over the keyboard, brought them down.

Here, in the isolated corner of the *Dark Star*, was the one place where he could create; the one place where he desired to produce and not destroy; the one place that reminded him even a little of home. This was his temple, his equivalent of Talby's dome, Boiler's picture-wall, Pinback's comic books.

Probably it was all the water. The blue rushing water —under him, over him, behind him. The friendly, familiar water lifting him up, up, and then sliding down the glassy green front. Always the blue-blue-green water.

His hands moved freely over the keys, loosening the final, flowing toccata from Widor's "Sixth Organ Concerto"—a piece of music at once as light and powerful as the deepest ocean swells. It rose up around him, engulfed the tiny room in sound and then in slick sliding wetness.

He played harder, faster now, riding the fugal structure to its foaming coda—the music building to a crescendo, one trill piling atop another as he kept treading the bass pedals. His toes dug into and became one with the smooth, well-waxed pedals as he slid down the front of the taut, smooth, vinyl-suited tossed crescendo which died slowly behind him . . .

He blinked.

The music was done. The ride was over. He was reborn, refreshed, cleansed, and whole again. One with the universe.

He hesitated, struck one awkwardly placed key. Somewhere within the flimsy maze a mallet or screwdriver moved to strike a jar partly filled with water. It made a dull, only vaguely musical sound.

He smiled to himself. Before the others he never smiled, but he could smile at himself here. It didn't matter that the organ played notes other from those he heard. He'd played the right board all along—the carefully waxed, hand-rubbed, delicately manipulated board, and the sounds had been real to him. He stood, surveyed the organ with pleasure.

A little of the water had evaporated. That was all. Just a little of the water.

He left the room.

Why couldn't the others understand? Pinback and Boiler, and even Powell. Even Powell had never understood what he saw in that "collection of splinters and junk" he persisted in calling an organ.

So the knowledge was Doolittle's and Doolittle's alone. That made him feel a little better, a little wiser than the others. But what about Talby? He frowned. Ho, Talby didn't understand the lieutenant's organ, either. His secret was safe.

Where was Talby's head right now, in fact? Doolittle checked his watch. Probably up in the dome, as usual. Doolittle turned on his heel, heading abruptly toward the food-preparation room instead of returning to their converted living quarters.

Once there, he dialed a major breakfast. Not for himself. For Talby. He would take it up to the astronomer, up to Talby in his serene contemplation of the heavens, and try to share his organ-ideas with him. Of all the crew, the astronomer might be able to understand.

There was a short pause, then nothing. The meals computer seemed reluctant to discharge a single breakfast at this hour. Doolittle pushed the activate-request switch repeatedly, until the machine finally coughed up the meal he had ordered. Then he headed for the observation dome access corridor.

He hesitated on his way up. Talby might not like

being disturbed. Doolittle thought about aborting this little expedition, but firmed himself. Talby might not like company, but even he had to eat.

Putting his head through the open hatch, he called softly, "Talby?"

There was a buzzing sound, and the chair spun around fast. Then Talby was staring down at him, his expression neutral.

"Here's some breakfast." He handed the slim metal package up to the astronomer. Talby took it, said nothing, but there was another buzz and the astronomer's cocoonlike chair slid back, making room for Doolittle in the confined space of the dome. It was Talby's way of welcoming him.

There was a little raised wedge on the far side of the hatch and Doolittle squeezed himself onto it, his feet framing either side of the opening. Like an upside-down well, light poured into the dome from the corridor below, lighting both faces from beneath. It gave Doolittle an uncharacteristically saturnine cast, while Talby, seated farther away, appeared wreathed in bloody shadows.

The lieutenant looked cautiously out through the dome. The universe wheeled around them. No, no, that was a phrase from a book. And it didn't apply. The universe was motionless, still, with a solemnity far more impressive than any slow motion.

They were moving, but even at their supreme speed the galaxy was too vast for any movement to be seen by the naked eye. Hyperspace was different, a comforting blur. You couldn't fear what you couldn't delineate.

But up here, with everything laid out sharp and uncompromising . . . Doolittle did not like coming up into the dome for too long. For a little while it was impressive, but after too long it began to weigh a man down with his own insignificance. Pinback and Boiler couldn't stand it for even a little while.

Even a little while was too long, and too long was—
Stop that, Doolittle. That's not healthy.

It was different back on Earth. He could remember liking it then. The universe had seemed a friendly place those nights, a magnificient tapestry of suns and nebulae woven solely as a proper background for the blue-white jewel of Earth as seen from the moon.

But Earth wasn't over his shoulder here. In their present position it was a distant pinprick of light which only the ship's computer could identify.

Oh, and Talby, of course. He hid his smile. Just like he claimed to be able to identify suns by sight, the astronomer persisted in claiming he could pick Sol out of the sky. That was impossible, considering all the course changes they had made in the lost, gone years.

But if asked, Talby would unhesitatingly point to some point in the sky and say, "Sol? There it is. But why do you want to know? It's not a very important star." And he would return to his solemn study of the surrounding heavens.

Doolittle didn't really know why being up in the dome for a while bothered him. It shouldn't have. That was one thing he didn't have to lie about—he had shown no symptoms of space fear. Fear of the great open spaces between the stars.

No, the vastnesses of the galaxy supposedly held no terrors for him. But then, the psychologists who had told him that hadn't spent years floating away from sight of Earth in a tiny metal triangle, years without even a glimpse of their own sun. A journey like this brought home to a man something about space no psychometrician could ever approximate.

Not that it was complicated. No. Space was big, man was small, and you couldn't dwell on that very long or the bigness would assume its proper proportions and come down on the mind and smash it. But Talby, he reflected, seemed to have licked that problem. He was going to turn some theories around when he got back home, if they could ever pry him out of his precious dome. Talby thrived on the emptiness.

Doolittle hated him for it.

Talby had removed his headset and was ripping the protective foil off his breakfast. Wadding up the thin metal into a ball, he tossed it with casual unconcern down the open hatchway. Doolittle followed its path until it had vanished from sight, then he turned his gaze back on the astronomer, who was starting to suck on a tube of concentrated eggs.

"You know, Talby, you really ought to come down and eat your meals with the rest of us. Or at least come down to sleep. You spend too much time up here."

At least a thousand times now he had repeated similar statements of identical content to the astronomer. And for the thousandth time Talby, as unperturbed as ever, came back with the same answer—after swallowing a mouthful of food.

"Why? I like it up here. I don't bother any of you, do I? You should be glad of the extra privacy."

"We've got plenty of privacy, Talby. We've got a whole ship that's almost empty now in which to hide from each other." He paused, then went on in a different vein. "You used to come down and eat with the rest of us. Doesn't it get lonely being up here so much? I mean, privacy is one thing, Talby, but . . ."

He trailed off as the astronomer finished his eggs. Finished them quickly, Doolittle thought. In a hurry to get the awkward refueling of his body out of the way. That wasn't natural. Mealtime was one of their few remaining ties to Earthly habits. Talby opened a tube of bread substitute.

"I don't like going below since Commander Powell died," he said. "I feel too enclosed down there."

"Yeah," muttered Doolittle helplessly. What could he say to that? "You should spend more time below, though. You know, see more of the ship."

"Me?" Talby answered, hearing him and yet not hearing him. "What do I want to look at the ship for? I know what the ship looks like. That's not why I came on this mission, Doolittle." He leaned back and stared outward with that peculiar, farsighted stare Doolittle now knew instantly.

"Up here, I can watch things, Doolittle. I love to watch things. Just stare at the sun systems and nomad meteors, gas clusters and distant galaxies. You know, I bet I've seen more stars than any human being alive, Doolittle. And you never know what may come tumbling by to say hello in overdrive or hyperdrive. Some of them would surprise you, Doolittle."

"Yeah," Doolittle mumbled again. Talby was making him increasingly nervous these days. "But you'll have plenty of time for that later, though. I mean, think of it this way: we've been in space twenty years now and we've only aged three years physically, so there'll be plenty of time later for staring around. Won't there, Talby? Talby?"

"Are we really going into the Veil Nebula region?" the astronomer whispered.

"Of course we are," Doolittle insisted. "I mean, I gave the order and supervised the course correction, didn't I? It's programmed, isn't it?"

"You know, Doolittle," Talby said quietly, "if we are going into the Veil region, we may actually find a strange and beautiful thing: the Phoenix Asteroids. They should be passing through there about now, if the predictions are really correct."

"Oh. Phoenix Asteroids." Doolittle's brow furrowed. It seemed to him that that was a name he should know, a name he'd heard before. It wasn't that he'd cheated his way through the astronomy courses, too. It was just that he hadn't paid much attention to anything but the basics for navigation and plotting. Sightseeing highlights he had kind of glossed over.

"Phoenix Asteroids?" he confessed finally. "I don't think I ever heard of them."

Talby gave him a look Doolittle couldn't quite interpret. Anger. Contempt. Pity.

"They're a body of asteroids—at least, that's what the best guesses think they are—that are running on a definite orbit, but one so vast that for years nobody could calculate it.

"They were detected right after the development of the first big lunar telescopes. They don't travel in a straight line like most asteroid groupings. Nor do they belong to any one sun system. But they have a true orbit.

"Once every twelve point three trillion years they circle our universe. They pass through our galaxy in the region of Sol just once, and they'll return in slightly less than twelve point three trillion years from now. But the Earth won't be here to meet them. The Earth may not be anyplace by then. The universe may not be anyplace. But the Phoenix will."

"Crazy . . . how can anybody calculate an orbit like that?" muttered Doolittle, and then he felt stupid for asking it because, obviously, somebody *had* calculated it.

"I don't know, Doolittle. I'm no computer, but it's been done. As for the Phoenix itself, we don't know much about it. Its composition is just a guess. An asteroidal grouping seems as logical as anything for something that defies as many laws as this does." He leaned back in his chair and looked outward, outward. The Phoenix Asteroids . . .

. "They're something different, Doolittle. Something so different we can't even begin to assign an explanation for them. For example, for the scopes on the moon to pick them up visually means they must have their own internal source of light, Doolittle, and an incredibly intense one at that. They glow. Their spectrum changes constantly, the colors on the charts flow like wine. Nobody knows how, or why. By rights, an astronomical object that small should be invisible to us at such distances. You shouldn't be able to detect them from Earth at all, let alone distinguish something like color. But you can, Doolittle, you can."

Doolittle just stared at Talby, thinking. It seemed to him that he would remember something as spectacular as the Phoenix Asteroids, despite his often lackadaisical approach to some courses. Were they real . . . or another figment of Talby's all-too-active imagination, the product of too much stimulation from an unrelenting universe viewed too long?

"They just glow," Talby was whispering as he stared out the dome, "just glow as they drift in a great grand circle around the whole universe. The Phoenix Asteroids."

Doolittle considered what Talby had said for a long time, while neither man said anything. The only sounds were occasional ship groans and mechanical belches rumbling up through the open hatch.

Doolittle finally looked up, hands folded in front of him, and spoke to Talby. "You know what I think about, Talby? You're always talking about yourself, and Boiler and Pinback let themselves go any old time—but I'm not like that. Yet up here . . ." and he gazed at the heavens above, "it's easier to talk, I think. You know what I think about?"

The astronomer didn't respond, but looked expectantly down at him. Thus encouraged, Doolittle talked on, his hands twisting and turning on themselves.

"It's funny . . . I kinda sit around a lot on the ship, alone, trying to get a lotta time to myself. I can't talk to the others, really. I've never been too good at talking to anybody in the program. I don't know why. It bothers me, Talby. I didn't have any trouble talking to people back home. I was positively gregarious, back home."

"We've all gone through a change, Doolittle," Talby said in a sepulchral voice.

"Yeah, I guess . . . Anyway, with time to myself, I can think about back . . . back home in Malibu. Do you know where Malibu is, Talby?"

The astronomer shook his head. Mere Terran geography held little interest for him. His cartographic concerns were cosmic in scope.

"It's a little town north of Los Angeles Megalopolis. A beach town. I lived there before I got into the program. And I used to surf all the time, Talby. I used to be a great surfer." He paused, glanced up at the silent astronomer. "What time do you think it is back home, Talby, back in the States?"

Talby stared out the dome. "In Los Angeles, it would be about eight-oh-five in the morning."

"Yes, sure." Doolittle tried to hide his smile. "But what time of year?"

Talby shook his head.

"I'll bet it's spring," Doolittle mused, his smile spreading. "The waves at Malibu and Zuma—that's a beach north of Malibu, Talby—are so fantastic in the spring. I can remember running down the beach in those early spring mornings in my wet suit, my board under my arm and the fog pricking my face . . ." He stopped. Talby wasn't really listening. He was watching the stars again. But it was good to talk to someone else about it.

"The waves would really be peaking, you know . . . high and glassy." He might have been describing a woman now—and in a sense, he was. "You'd hit that water, just smash into it, and before you could wake up you're coming right off one of those walls and you just ride all the way in, perfect."

"Perfect," Talby echoed, looking back down at him suddenly. Maybe a part of him had been listening after all.

"You know," the lieutenant continued sadly, "I guess I miss the waves and my board more than anything."

Talby smiled. "Tell me more about it, Doolittle."

"You really want to hear?"

Talby nodded, and Doolittle told him about the waves . . .

4

PINBACK SHIFTED AWKWARDLY in the beach lounge chair and adjusted his sunglasses. It was hot on the sand today. He squinted up at the brilliant sun directly overhead.

Judging by the position of Old Sol, it was just about noontime. He'd have to get ready for lunch—but not yet. The sun felt too good right now. He glanced at his watch. Have to be careful; another ten minutes on this side and then he'd turn over and bake the other half.

Leaning back, he squirmed into a comfortable position on the lounge, fiddling slightly with his swimsuit and tank top. Just another ten minutes.

He was slipping into a comfortable half-dreamworld when the scratching sound interrupted. He tried to ignore it, but it refused to go away. Not only that, but it was getting louder. Now what?

Must be some kid nearby digging with a shovel. Have to speak to his mother. Pinback raised his glasses, leaned out from under the glare of the big sunlamp, and glanced back up the narrow corridor.

Boiler's backside hove into view, out of place and unwelcome, thoroughly shattering the idle illusion Pinback had so carefully constructed. The corporal was dragging something heavy in the artifical gravity, a large, square piece of metal with open hinges on one side.

Pinback thought he recognized it. He watched as Boiler dragged the weighty slab over to the far end of the corridor and turned it, leaning it at an angle up against the wall, facing back at them. Then he did recognize it.

"Hey, that's the lid to the heating unit, isn't it?"

Boiler ignored him. He examined the lid, then knelt and readjusted it so that it rested against the wall at a slightly sharper angle. Then he rubbed his hands in evident satisfaction and walked back past Pinback.

The sergeant watched him leave. He was as puzzled as he was awake, now. Boiler's cryptic activities seemed to have no meaning. Pinback was enlightened moments later.

Boiler reappeared and now held a large, cumbersome object cradled tightly in both arms. Even though they had used this particular instrument only once before, and a long time ago at that, Pinback knew what it was immediately.

It was the portable laser—both lighter and deadlier than it looked. Its presence in Boiler's hands suggested unpleasant possibilities.

For a moment Pinback thought of just leaving. When Boiler got some crazy idea fixed in his Neanderthal skull, nobody could talk him out of it. Not even Doolittle. And whatever he was up to now was bound to be crazier than most.

He took a step toward the exit, then stopped. This wasn't something he could just walk away from. If Boiler wanted to try to mutilate his own hand with his collection of knives, that was one thing. But the laser was more than a toy.

"You're . . . you're not supposed to have that out except in an emergency," he finally managed to stutter. His beach fantasy had long since been shattered. "That's not for target practice."

Boiler barely bothered to glance at him. Instead, he hefted the weapon and lined up an eye with the lens-sight. While Pinback watched and fretted, Boiler pulled the trigger.

There was a short burst of intolerably bright red light. The light beam contacted the center of the propped-up lid. A brief flare of flame erupted from the wounded area as the intense heat ignited the metal itself. It died out quickly, cooling.

A neat hole surrounded by molten metal had been drilled in the lid's middle. Boiler looked back at Pinback and smiled with pleasure. Then he licked his thumb and touched it to the sight at the far end of the laser, a backwoodsman's gesture of centuries past.

"That's dangerous," Pinback insisted inanely as the corporal raised the laser again. "You might cut all the way through the lid and into the ship's circuitry. You could cut through something vital."

Boiler fired again. There was a puff of white from the lid this time as another hole spurted tiny flames and appeared alongside the first. Boiler frowned, lowered the weapon, and began adjusting some switches set into one side.

Pinback watched him nervously, wishing Powell, wishing even Doolittle were here. He really should go and get Doolittle, but what would Boiler do if left alone?

"Suppose you cut right through the lid and then through the hull of the ship? What about that, huh?"

"Oh, for heaven's sake, it's calibrated for distance, stupid," Boiler growled.

"So what? You could still make a mistake. It wouldn't take much. I'll tell Doolittle."

Boiler's head jerked up, and he stared dangerously at the sergeant. Boiler was right on the edge, and something just might have happened except—

They were interrupted by a smooth, faintly erotic voice that was totally unexpected right then.

"Sorry to break in on your recreation, fellows," the computer announced contritely, "but it is time for Sergeant Pinback to feed the alien."

"Awwww," Pinback groaned, shuffling one foot and looking down at the floor, "I don't wanna do that now."

"May I remind you, Sergeant Pinback," the computer continued inexorably, "that it was your idea in the first place, and no one else's, to bring the alien on board. If I may quote you, you said, 'the ship needs a mascot.' "

"Yeah, but—" Pinback tried to protest. The computer rode over any obje tions.

"It was your idea, so looking after it is your responsibility, Sergeant Pinback."

Boiler gave him the sinister ha-ha.

"Rats," grumbled Pinback. "I've gotta do everything around here. It's everybody's mascot—why can't they help out?"

"It's your pet, buddy. I don't even like looking at it. Gives me the galloping quivers. Even Doolittle thinks you should toss it out the lock."

"No feelings, any of you. So it isn't the perfect pet, so what? We all have our faults."

Boiler greeted that with another ha-ha and turned back to adjusting the laser.

Pinback walked off down the corridor muttering to himself. Lazy, care-for-nothings, insensitive—a good thing at least one person on this ship was interested in something besides destruction. Wait till they got back to Earth and everyone got a look at *his* alien. Not much question who would get the medals then! He had intended to share the glory with the others, but if they didn't care enough to help look after it, well then, they could just go find their own mascots!

He muttered to himself in this manner all the way back to the compartment they had sealed off for the live alien specimens. On the way he stopped and picked up a dustpan and broom. A sanitary portable vacuum would have been more practical and more efficient, but some insane psychometrician back on Earth had decided that a dustpan and broom would be the better choice.

They'd feel less lonely with a few familiar tools around, and the extra exercise would be desirable. Pinback wished the psycher were there now, so he could exercise the dustpan and broom over his skull.

Over door was a crude stenciled sign that read

WATCH IT! The admonition had firm foundation in previous happenings, and he opened the door carefully.

His particular pet alien had grown more and more adventurous as it had become acclimated to the ship. The last time he had gone to look after it, it had been waiting just inside the doorway to pounce on him.

Then there was the time the luminants had gotten loose. Brilliantly hued geometric shapes of pure light, the most alien life form they had ever encountered, the luminants had allowed themselves to be docilely convoyed on board and into a cage of lucite. Once in free space, they had proceeded to saunter out of their "cage" as though it were not there—which for them was quite true. There followed a hectic week of pursuing them all over the ship, with dark panels, flashlights, and anything they thought might induce or force the luminants back into their cage.

It was all frantic and impossible. How do you capture something made out of pure light? It was Powell who finally hit on the idea of using mirrors. A complex arrangement of hidden mirrors made their new cage into an honest one. They could still slip out any time they wanted—but the internal mirror arrangement insisted otherwise. So they stayed put, inside the glass prison.

Pinback stepped into the room and quickly looked around. No sign of the Beachball.

The room was empty except for the luminants' big smoked-glass cage. Four of the luminants responded immediately to his presence. Pity they weren't intelligent. They were peaceful, even friendly—and extremely stupid.

Now, as he hunted for the Beachball, the four light-creatures floated close to the glass wall of their cage. They might have made nice pets . . . but how could you pet a thing you couldn't even be sure was there? It would have been like trying to be affectionate to the beam of a searchlight.

Pinback didn't like them.

"All right, where are you?" He bent over and started peering under tilted crates and empty shelves. "Come on, ball, quit playing around." Beachball was an accurate description, if not a particularly dignified name for the alien. Boiler, typically, had named it, and despite Pinback's best efforts to the contrary, the label had stuck.

It was better than naming it after Pinback, which had been the corporal's initial suggestion. At first Pinback was flattered. Then, as the nature of the alien became more obvious, he was considerably less so.

"Come on, quit hidin'." The luminants swarmed over to the side of the cage nearest him, and he waved his arms irritably at them. "Go on, beat it."

They scattered to the back of the cage. Even their total alienness could be tolerated if they would only make a *sound* of some sort—something to indicate a bare hint of the sentience that was probably there.

"Come on, come," he muttered. He set the broom and pan down on a huge crate and started snapping his fingers. "I haven't got time for this. Come on."

There was a sudden flash of spotted red in front of him, followed by a loud thump. Startled, Pinback jumped back. Then he recognized the source of the sound. He put hands on hips and glared down at the alien angrily, covering his nervousness. "And to think when I brought you on the ship I thought you were cute."

The alien twittered enigmatically back at him.

Well, to a man who had been away from home and all other companionship save that of his crewmates for as many years as Pinback had, the alien *might* have seemed cute at one time.

It was about a third the size of a grown man, neatly spherical, and colored bright red. Large blotches of yellow, black, and green concentric circles mottled the pulsing body. It also sported a set of clawed, lightly webbed feet. That was all. It possessed nothing resembling hands, arms, a multipart torso, or even a face.

It could distinguish sounds and sight, though the organs carrying out these functions were well hidden beneath the bulbous body. Occasionally it made sounds like a querulous canary. These were matched by deeper moans which sounded suspiciously like Pinback sounded when he had a bad bellyache.

The sergeant had moved to a nearby cabinet and was rummaging inside it. After a bit he came out with a large, somewhat frayed head of alien-world cabbage. They had run out of food from the alien's own home world a long time ago, its appetite proving to be far greater than even Pinback could have imagined.

"All right, soup's on." He held out the battered greenery. "Come on, this is no time to get picky. We don't have any more of the other stuff."

The alien made no move to come forward. "Here, eat it," Pinback yelled. He tossed the vegetable toward the alien. He was about fed up with this "pet."

The cabbage bounced a couple of times and came to a stop in front of the Beachball.

"Eat it, damn you. Take it or leave it. It's all we've got."

The alien seemed to pause, then leaned forward over the food as if inspecting it with invisible eyes. Both multiple claws tapped at the floor, an imitation of a gesture it had observed in Pinback. Whether or not the alien had any real intelligence was questionable, though at times it performed actions apparently unexplainable in any other way. But that it was imitative, like a parrot, was undeniable. Certainly it hadn't displayed anything which could be interpreted as an effort toward communication.

Eventually the tapping stopped. The claws reached out, grabbed the cabbage, and shoved it back toward Pinback. It twittered noisily.

"Oh yeah? What am I supposed to do now, huh? Whip you up a twelve-course RD-Three gourmet dinner? I don't know anything about the kind of food you like. These old specimen vegetables are the only nonconcentrates we've got aboard, and I don't think you would like concentrates—we're not crazy about them ourselves."

The Beachball quivered, twittered mindlessly.

"Ah, go ahead," Pinback finally said disgustedly, turning his back on the alien and picking up the broom and dustpan. "Starve—see if I care." He started muttering to himself again. "Do all the work . . . damn unappreciative alien twit . . ."

Moving on short, powerful little legs, the alien took a leap and jumped onto the cabinet to Pinback's right. It might have been trying to draw his attention. If so, it failed. Pinback continued to sweep, gathering alien excrement into the dustpan.

"I do my best to prepare your meals, I clean up after you, and do you appreciate it?" He snorted, spotted another dirty area, and swept again.

The alien paused at its post on the cabinet and appeared to consider the situation. Either it had a definite plan in mind, or else Pinback's bent-over form was just too tempting a situation. It leaped.

Twittering violently, it landed, claws first, square on Pinback's back. Pinback yelped and straightened up, but the Beachball hung on, scratching and bouncing ferociously against him.

"Hey, come on," Pinback yelled, dropping both the pan and broom and trying to swat behind himself. "Get off . . . get offa my back, damnit!" But while the alien was large and didn't weigh much, it was also smooth-surfaced and extremely difficult to get a grip on. Pinback couldn't.

"All right . . . all right, now," he shouted, "that's enough! Come off it. That's—hey!"

The alien had shifted its position slightly higher onto his back and now was in position to pull at Pinback's shoulder-length tresses.

"My hair . . . quit pulling my . . . ouch!"

He staggered, aware for the first time that the Beachball might not be playing now. Still clawing at the thing on his back, he stumbled into a wall, turned, and staggered away. The alien reached around and started to paw his face.

Now frantic, Pinback finally managed to get a hand between himself and the alien and shoved it free. Immediately the being fell off, bounced on the floor, and scampered out the open door while twittering loosely in what might have been interpreted as a pleased fashion.

"Goddamn son-of-a-bitch, ungrateful, stupid, rotten, alien tomato-thing!" Pinback finally got the hair out of his eyes, then moved to the door and peeked out into the corridor.

It was sitting about halfway up the hall, panting like a happy puppy and, despite the absence of obvious eyes, no doubt watching him intently. Pinback sighed.

Well, the thing just wanted to play, after all. "All right, fun is fun. Get back in here." He stepped into the corridor and started toward it, snapping his fingers. "Come on, come on." The alien didn't budge.

"Come on now . . . good boy . . . good Beachball . . . that's right." He was closing in on it. Now he leaned forward to give it a reassuring stroke— and it made a violent lunge at him. Despite its not having a mouth in sight, or teeth, Pinback drew his hand away fast.

He knew enough about alien life-forms now to realize that it might have other, less visible but nonetheless potent, forms of defense.

Those unattractive yellow and black spots, for example, occasionally showed suspicious signs of moisture around the rims. Maybe the alien could secrete something unpleasant when angered. Why, it might even be toxic; and here they had been harboring it all these weeks.

Come to think of it, nobody *had* run any extensive tests on the alien. It had seemed so friendly and blatantly harmless at first that the thought had not occurred to him—or to anyone else. He sort of regretted that little oversight, because now he didn't know whether the Beachball was bluffing or not.

Its claws were another proposition entirely, of course, though his skin was more irritated than broken.

Well, he wasn't going to take any chances. Its twittering as it had lunged at him had risen to a sound that bore more than casual resemblance to a growl.

If it did just want to play, he was going to have to try something else to get control over it. Perhaps the subtle approach.

It ought to be inside his jumpsuit . . . ah, there. This had always worked with the creature before. He leaned over cautiously, shoved the object toward the Beachball, and squeezed it.

It was a tiny gray mouse with pink ears and a big pink nose. It made satisfying squeaking sounds. These didn't seem especially erudite to Pinback, but maybe they were close to Beachball talk. He squeezed it again.

"Here, boy . . . want the mousey? Nice mousey, pretty mousey . . ." This was a helluva occupation for a grown technician. "Want your mouse? Here, boy."

The Beachball didn't appear inclined to move any closer, but the violent pulsing seemed to lessen. Pinback dropped the rubber toy just in front of it. Again the claws tapped on the floor in imitation (or was it imitation?) of Pinback.

Coming to some Beachballian decision, the alien took a short hop forward and covered the mouse. Non-twittering sounds began to issue from it—crunching, swallowing sounds. Pinback interpreted them correctly. The alien was eating the mouse.

"Idiot!" he screamed, and reached down to recover the mouse's remains.

The Beachball lunged forward again and this time made contact with Pinback's bare hand. There was a searing sensation as if he had waved his hand over a low flame, and the alien almost hissed at him. Pinback jerked away, holding his hand and sucking at the injured member to try and lessen the pain—a purely reflexive, not too bright action on his part. Fortunately, the substance had already sunk into the skin and so didn't transfer to his tongue.

So much for subtlety and psychology. Now it was time for less Freudian approaches.

He disappeared inside the alien-holding room, and reemerged moments later hefting the broom firmly in one hand. It would have been easier with someone else to help herd the Beachball, but Boiler would only have laughed and he doubted that the oh-so-superior Doolittle would have bothered.

It didn't matter. He could handle the alien by himself. He'd show the others he could. Turning up the corridor, he prepared to give it fair warning . . . and stopped.

The alien had disappeared.

It still wanted to play? All right! He started up the corridor, looking behind him at every odd second. You had to watch out for the alien. It was tricky. Not intelligent, but tricky. There was a definite animal cunning in that Beachball. It reminded him of Boiler.

He slowed as he approached the turn in the corridor, edged cautiously up to it—and peered quickly around the bend. Not . . . something grabbed his ankles, and he screamed. But this time the alien had made a mistake. While it had a solid grip with both clawed feet, its muscular system was weak and it couldn't put much into the grip. Certainly not enough to topple Pinback.

The sergeant turned at the waist and swatted downward with the broom, catching the alien squarely.

It twittered and let go, backing away down the corridor, back, back. Pinback followed, continuing to swat at it. He had driven it halfway back to the holding-room entrance when the Beachball apparently decided it had taken enough.

Timing its leap in midswing, it caught the broom handle right at the base of the plastic straw and yanked it from Pinback's grasp. Now, using its semi-flying ability, it showed its imitative tendencies once again by flailing violently at Pinback, forcing him back down the corridor.

"No, no . . . you idiot . . . ow, yowch!" Something caught his feet and he stumbled, the broom crashing down heavily on the back of his neck.

"No, no!" Pinback continued to flail about for a couple of seconds until he suddenly realized that the broom was no longer in belligerent motion. He grabbed at it, glanced up, and saw the alien disappearing around the far end of the corridor.

It was moving back toward the engine-service area, the rear of the ship.

Not that he was worried about anything as theatrical as a suddenly sapient alien taking over the ship, but if the mischievous monster got itself entangled in any delicate machinery . . .

Naturally, anything that could be easily damaged should be well protected. But considering the lapse of maintenance on the ship these last months, there was no telling what shielding panels or covers might be out of place. No telling what Boiler might have played with besides the heat-unit shielding. The sooner the alien was back in its room and locked up, the better.

Untangling himself from the broom, Pinback started down the corridor after the rambunctious alien. One open bay after another yielded nothing. He was about to start back when a familiar twittering sound came to him from one of the big service bays. He moved slowly inside.

The twittering seemed to come from just behind the door leading to the inner service chamber. He put a hand on the latch, at the same time wondering that the creature had had enough sense or curiosity to close it behind itself, and threw it open.

Nothing showed inside but a tangle of old machinery, dimly lit by the service lights. Hunting through the room, broom firmly in hand, he followed the faint honking. The sound was moving away from him again, and the darkness was increasing. There wasn't much reason to visit this part of the ship.

The section he was heading for was fully automatic and he wouldn't find much of anything in the way of lighting there. He'd have to bring his own light with him.

There was a powerful flashlight in one of the service boxes. It produced a satisfyingly broad beam. Aiming it ahead and sweeping it thoroughly into all deep corners, he moved deeper into the little-visited service section of the ship.

This was absolutely crazy. There were never sup-

posed to be fewer than two men at a time in this section
of the *Dark Star*. There were too many things that needed two sets of hands to repair, and a number of things
that could go bang at odd moments. But Pinback had
forgotten most of that. Over the years, you only remembered the parts of the ship that had given you trouble.

Also, a number of elevator and ventilation shafts ran
through here at odd angles. But there was no danger of
stumbling into one of those, not with the light. Actually,
he had no business being this deep into the service bay
by himself. It was strictly againt regs. But he couldn't
tell Doolittle what had happened, not now. And he
didn't dare tell Boiler.

No, Doolittle would have given him another of those
supercontemptuous smiles which he reserved only for
Pinback. And Boiler—Boiler would either grin or,
worse, laugh outright. But he could tell Talby. So someone would know where he was.

He hesitated. Talby might understand—but for sure
he wouldn't do anything to help. So why bother? Pinback moved on. Crazy Talby. At least he was harmless.
Not like Boiler, who—

There was a twittering sound to his right, and he
swung the beam rapidly in that direction. The brilliant,
slick red epidermis of the Beachball gleamed back at
him.

It was sitting in a small square doorway. Pinback
didn't recognize it right away—and when he did, his
breath came up short. The alien was sitting in this level's
emergency entrance to the main service-elevator shaft.

Maybe he could pry it into the room. He jabbed at it
with the broom, but it was impossible to get the end of
the stick behind the alien. Suddenly it moved—backward, into the shaft. Pinback dropped to all fours and
crawled forward quickly. There was a chance he could
reach it with the stick before it drifted down too far.

Holding the flashlight in front of him, he had just a
quick glimpse of the Beachball as it vanished through
the open hatchway on the *other* side of the shaft.

He sat back, sighed. Now he was really in trouble.

The alien was loose in one of the most sensitive, least-visited areas of the *Dark Star*. It could roam around back there, fooling with who knew what, unless it was recaptured immediately.

But he had no way to get across the shaft. If he could only bring the elevator down it would be easy enough to cross over its top and slip through the emergency hatchway the alien had just vacated.

But the elevator was locked and could be activated only at the expense of notifying those on the bridge that it was in use. If he slipped back there and keyed it himself, certainly Doolittle or Boiler would be on station. And if they saw the elevator suddenly thrown into use, they would want to know what Pinback was doing fussing around in a section of the ship he had no business visiting.

If he remembered correctly, use of the elevator would even key a warning light in their living quarters. Only when it was working on automatic was the signal silent. And no sound issued from the shaft now.

He didn't think he could concoct an excuse that would fool Doolittle. Eventually he would end up confessing that he had let the alien escape. Then he would be in terrible shape. Doolittle wouldn't trust him with *anything,* and Boiler would never stop snickering.

All right, so he wouldn't use the elevator. He would get the alien back without anyone knowing, and without anyone's help. He stuck his head into the shaft, looked across, then down. It would help it he weren't so afraid of heights. He could drift in a starsuit for hours without being troubled, but he got dizzy atop a ladder.

Not that it was so terribly far from here to the bottom of the shaft. The *Dark Star* wasn't that big. If he slipped and fell while trying to cross, why, he might only break an arm or maybe both legs. In addition to being painful, that would be even worse than asking for Doolittle's or Boiler's help—but he was going to get across.

With what? There was nothing like an emergency ladder going down the shaft. The elevator was equipped with too many fail-safes—there was no need for a ladder. And there was no other way to the rear of the ship except across this shaft.

It had been designed this way, on the off chance that if any crewmember went berserk and tried to kick himself out the emergency airlock, or fool with the vital communications/life-support instrumentation, he would have to use the elevator—thus activating those tell-tales in the bridge and living quarters that now bedeviled Pinback.

No one could use the elevator without some other member of the crew knowing about it. But Pinback would fool them—somehow.

Moving back into the service chamber, he hunted around with the light. Eventually he found a heavy metal canister which he was sure the wiry but light alien wouldn't be able to move. He rolled it over until it blocked the small hatchway.

Then he hurried back up to the crafts room. It was empty. Doolittle's wooden-jar organ sat alone, silent, behind a thin partition. The pottery wheels, the glass works, the metal etching and macrame sections, the instructional film viewers—all were deserted. That meant Doolittle and Boiler were either forward in the control room or, more likely, relaxing in their living quarters. Good. It didn't matter to Pinback whether they were taking sunlamp treatments or a bath—as long as they were out of his way.

A short search, and he found what he was looking for—a good long solid board, designed for carving and therapeutic woodwork, now to be put to a purely practical use. He hurried down the corridor with it.

The canister was still in place, with no sign that the alien had tired to force it. That meant it was still on the other side.

Sweating, Pinback heaved the canister aside and peered across the dark elevator shaft. Still no sign of the alien, neither in the black unlit depths nor in the heights above.

Carefully, working as noiselessly as possible, he edged the board across the open gap. His one real concern was that it might not be long enough, but it spanned the gulf easily.

It would have been nice if he had had a board more than a dozen centimeters wide. This was not a very reassuring bridge, but it would have to do. And it was much better than a cable, which for a while he thought he might have to use.

Well, there was nothing left but simply to climb on and crawl across. Nothing to it. His pulse was racing.

Come on, now, Pinback, it's only a couple of meters. You'll be across before you know it.

Shifting the flashlight to his left hand, he put both hands out on the board, over the blackness, and pressed down sharply a couple of times. The board gave very slightly. Seemed solid enough.

Moving slowly, ever so slowly, he crawled out a centimeter at a time until his full weight was on the board. He stopped, jiggled while resting on the wood. Again it gave slightly. But there were no threatening cracking sounds, and the board didn't bend under him.

It was going to be all right.

Setting both hands in front of him, he brought his knees under his waist. Hands, knees, hands, knees—and then he was reaching for the far rim. He was more relieved than he cared to acknowledge when he was finally across and through the hatchway on the opposite side.

Standing up in the corridor, he saw lights in the distance. The only lights that would be shining here would be from the region of the emergency airlock, and then only if the interior airlock door had been activated.

Probably the crazy Beachball had bumbled into the contact switch which activated the door mechanism. Another couple of steps confirmed it. The door was wide open, the interior of the bay bright with light.

A sudden thought brought him to an abrupt stop. No doubt the alien was trapped inside. He had retreated to the absolute end of the ship. But Pinback had forgotten the broom. Well, he wasn't going back across that pit for a stick of wood. The flashlight would make do as a

prod. Considering his present state of mind, he suspected his bare hands would be equal to the job.

He slowed as he neared the open doorway, edged
right up to the opening, and jumped inside, holding the
flashlight in front of him and trying to scan every direction at once.

A familiar twittering and honking greeted him. The
alien was there, sure enough, clinging with those seemingly adhesive claws to the far wall. Pinback's gaze went
immediately to another nearby switch—the one that
would blow the explosive bolts on the emergency hatch
cover and send anyone inside the lock flying out into
free space.

Thus far the Beachball hadn't made a motion toward
it. But if it suddenly took it into its head—or wherever
its thinking mechanism was located—to fly onto the
switch, even its slight weight should be enough to set off
the device. He tried to edge toward it without being obvious.

"Go on, get out of there," he muttered menacingly,
dividing his gaze between the alien and the lock mechanism. He made poking motions toward the alien with
the blunt end of the flashlight. Unimpressed, the creature didn't budge.

"Out!" Pinback screamed. At his screech the alien
leaped, not for the worrisome switch but straight at Pinback. He should have been ready for it. He wasn't.

This time it didn't attempt to dig at him. Instead, it
made a sort of half-swipe in passing. That was more
than enough to distract Pinback. Then it flew out the
door, back the way they had both come.

Maybe now was the time to call for aid. After all, the
monster had made two recognizably antagonistic moves
at him. It could now be classed as definitely hostile, despite his earlier, gushing report. He saw his naiveté in
retrospect.

No, what kind of coward are you, Pinback? What are
you afraid of . . . a little corrosive alien saliva?

"Come back here, you!" he yelled decisively, hurrying in pursuit.

Actually, he made up some distance on it. But not enough. Reaching the hatchway leading to the shaft, he bent quickly, stared in—and saw the board disappearing back across the black gulf, back between a pair of busy clawed feet.

"No . . . oh, no . . ."

Beachball was being imitative again.

5

THEY RESTED LIKE that—man on one side, alien on the other. The alien gobbled playfully, evidently enjoying the interesting afternoon. It didn't *look* malicious. Pinback, however, found that he could no longer regard the alien with anything remotely like objectivity.

He sat on the inside of the access port, caught his breath, and thought. This was the end. Now he would have to go back to the emergency airlock, get on the intercom, and ask either Boiler or Doolittle to send the elevator down for him. No way he could even do that for himself now.

Turning and kneeling, he stared across the shaft at the alien. It was still resting on the edge of the drop, quivering expectantly and twittering to itself. Pinback eyed it and thought uncomplimentary thoughts.

He would never live this down. Never. Boiler would never let him forget it. If there were any way to avoid calling for help . . . but how? What else could he do?

The board was gone, and long wooden boards were not scattered haphazardly about the ship. If there were another way across the shaft . . .

Sure . . . . Leaning out, he looked down and traced the tiny ledge that ran completely around the interior walls. It was only a few centimeters wide, but it would hold his weight easily, being part of the structure itself.

If he moved carefully, took a step at a time, the ledge ought to be negotiable.

Unaware that his breathing had suddenly grown stronger than normal, he stuck his head, turned upward, into the shaft. Hanging on to the inside of the hatchway with both hands, he slid one foot out and tested the strength of the ledge. It was part of the shaft wall, for sure.

Gritting his teeth and edging his body out a little at a time, he soon found himself standing upright on the ledge, his body pressed tight against the wall, hands outstretched and facing inward.

He only looked down once.

Now, if he could just edge around, make his way across the first corner . . . Trying to get a grip on the smooth metal walls and wishing his members were as adhesive as the alien's seemed to be, he stepped over the first corner. Then the back foot, and he was already nearly halfway across.

Hell, this was easy! The Beachball gobbled at him, and Pinback felt secure enough to risk shaking a fist at it.

"Idiot! When I get out of here and get you back into your room—"

Another voice interrupted him sharply, and he looked wildly around the shaft.

"Attention, attention." Soft voice, feminine—the computer again. "The central trunk elevator shaft is now activated. All personnel please clear the area."

There was a snap, a brilliant flare, and the shaft suddenly appeared above and below him, fully lighted. Now he could see exactly how high it was, exactly how deep it was, and exactly where he was trapped in relationship to those extremes. He screamed. He was all right when he didn't have to look down and see a bottom, but now . . .

His fear quickly gave way to anger.

"Doolittle . . . Boiler, Talby. I'm in here, you idiots!

In the shaft. What are you playing with the elevator for? Turn it off. Turn . . . !"

His voice faded. There was absolutely no reason for Doolittle to activate the elevator. There was no reason for Boiler to activate the elevator. And even if there had been a reason for Talby to activate the elevator, he probably wouldn't have bothered. This led him to the obvious explanation: there had been another malfunction, possibly keyed by his own presence in the shaft.

Leaning back against the cool metal, he closed his eyes and worked at fighting his recalcitrant muscles. He couldn't stay here. One way or another, he had to get moving. Otherwise, when the elevator got to this level its bottom would peel him off the wall as neatly as old skin off a beach-burned back.

"Help!" he screamed again. *"Help!"*

Now stop that and save your breath, Pinback. There's nobody here to hear you, and nobody's coming to rescue you. You've got to get out of this by yourself.

He was nearly to the hatchway on the other side, but it was still occupied by the twittering form of the alien. Making sure he was well set on his left leg, he kicked at it with his right, trying to force the creature back into the chamber beyond.

The alien bounced up and down violently in the portal, obviously agitated, but not struck sufficiently to be hurt. Pinback kicked at it again, and added some curses for added punch.

"Get out of there, you . . . go on, get out, move, you ignorant, stupid, ungrate . . . !"

Making an especially virulent gobbling sound, the alien leaped—not backward, but into the shaft. It landed on Pinback's chest and immediately began scratching at him with its claws. The claws had little clutching power behind them, but it was still damned uncomfortable.

"No, no!" Flailing at it hysterically with both hands, he tried to beat it off without sacrificing his balance. He couldn't keep it up indefinitely. If it got to his eyes . . .

Somehow he spun on the narrow ledge. Now he had his stomach and face pressed up against the wall. But the sudden twist had only temporarily dislodged the alien. It simply jumped free and reattached itself, this time to his upper back.

"Get off, get off!"

Still beating at it with little success, he started edging toward his right. Maybe it would leave him if he went back into the old hatchway. Taking another step, he arched his back slightly and took a good swat at the Beachball with his right hand. At the same time, it made a particularly strong wrench at his right side.

There was a loud, gobbling scream—from Pinback —as he slipped. Both hands caught the ledge as he slumped down. He hung like that, dangling over the seemingly bottomless shaft. Well, it was far from bottomless. But it was far too far away for him to risk a drop.

Grunting and twisting, he fought to get one leg back up on the ledge, swinging his body from side to side without much luck.

The alien had hopped free at the moment of falling and was now comfortably ensconced once more in the hatchway. It appeared to regard Pinback with interest, quivering and honking in its maddeningly unconcerned fashion.

Pinback had no trouble holding on—he'd been something of a gymnast in secondary school. No doubt with a little more effort he could get back up. At least, he thought so until he felt a frighteningly familiar light pressure on his shoulder blades.

"No . . . oh, no . . . I don't want to play anymore. Get off. Get offfff!"

The alien's weight was negligible. Its activities were not. After several moments of serene sizing-up, it started to squeeze at Pinback's rib cage. The sergeant started to scream, but soon found himself laughing uncontrollably. Occasionally the laugh would dissolve into a scream for help.

"Stop . . . s-s-stop! That's not . . . f-funny!" The alien continued its merciless tickling.

It shouldn't have known what it was doing—certainly

Pinback couldn't recall any time when he'd done any tickling, or been tickled, in the alien's presence. He might have forgotten something, though.

In any case, he had no time to ponder the possibilities of a carefully camouflaged alien intelligence suddenly coming to the surface. The tickling was weakening him in a way that hanging on couldn't. At least nothing more could happen.

A mechanical voice drifted through the shaft.

"Attention, attention . . ."

"Arrghh . . . no!" Pinback howled.

"Elevator descending for midweekly proficiency check. Please clear the shaft."

"You crazy bundle of crossed circuits—this isn't midweek!"

"Your cooperation will be appreciated."

Pinback's gaze turned wildly upward. His laughter and his grip on the narrow ledge were fading fast. There was a muffled clank, followed by a whirring sound.

Above him, a smooth white panel began to grow larger—the bottom of the slowly descending elevator. His eyes widened. "Goddamn it!" Tears began to start from them, half from laughter, half from desperation.

Making a supreme effort, he somehow managed to get both arms up onto the ledge at the same time. This seemed to catalyze something in the Beachball's mind. Whether bored with the tickling or disappointed at its lack of success in getting Pinback to let go, or for some incomprehensible reason known only to animated Beachballs, the creature floated free and jumped back into the hatchway.

With a smooth whine to indicate that all its components were functioning perfectly, the elevator continued to descend, a wide white foot coming down to crush Pinback.

He struggled wildly, got his foot, then his right leg back onto the ledge. Now that the alien had decided to leave him alone, his strength was coming back. Fighting frantically, he managed to get himself onto the ledge. Hands pressed against the wall, he started to stand.

He was just taking a retreating step toward the hatchway when the elevator touched his face—and stopped. Having detected interference, the lift would pause for a second, then move downward in stages unless it encountered stiff resistance. Pinback would not supply stiff resistance.

It would peel him off the ledge in slow jerks.

Even as he thought, the elevator dropped another tenth of a meter, bunching up his face and shoving him backward so that he was arching over the shaft. Another drop, and it would be impossible for him to keep his balance.

Just to one side of his scrunched-up face he saw a single metal bar suspended from the bottom of the lift. Reaching for it desperately, he just got a hand around it when the elevator dropped again.

Swinging out into open space, he grabbed with the other hand, rested in open air as the elevator slid another notch downward. That last one would have sent him tumbling down the shaft. His present position would not last forever, either, but it was better than lying broken fifty or sixty meters below.

There was a soft click, the pitch of the whining motor changed slightly, and he found himself rising as the elevator started up. He'd had some vague hope that it would continue downward until he could drop free. Now he dared not.

"Help . . . for God's sake, somebody, help!"

No one heard him, of course. And no doubt the malfunctioning elevator was stimulating no red warning light in the control room, so no one would be hurrying back here to check it out.

He wondered what the damn elevator would do next. How long did one of these automatic proficiency tests last, anyhow? It couldn't keep going up and down, up and down, forever—though it showed no sign of stopping.

There was no logic to it. Like the rest of the instrumentation on the *Dark Star,* it was operating in a typically haphazard manner.

As for the alien—he looked upward, and if he twisted his body, so, he could just see around one edge of the elevator. There was a brief flash of red, which had to be the Beachball clearing the shaft with ease. It squeezed through the other side, and as Pinback passed that level, with its open hatchways—open, unreachable hatchways—he saw it scampering along back to where he had disturbed it. Back to the emergency airlock.

Imitative creatures have one other characteristic in common with man—they are intensely curious. If Pinback had gone to the trouble of trying to root it out of the place it had been exploring, then it followed that there must be something in that place of particular interest to Beachballs. Anyhow, it was no longer curious about Pinback, now dangling helplessly in the shaft behind it.

The room certainly was an interesting place, though we have no descriptive referents capable of explaining exactly how the alien saw it. It was full of control panels, switches, blinking lights, five ranked sets of starsuits.

The Beachball examined each in turn, bouncing over open shelves and packages of emergency foodstuffs and even the triple knob that Pinback had sweated over—the one which, if engaged, would blow open the outer emergency door, an event that would be disastrous to anyone on the lock side of an airtight portal.

Not that the Beachball knew or could comprehend any of this. In any case, it elected not to play with the triple knob. Instead, its attention was drawn to a partial hole in the wall, where a protective plate had come loose and now swung from a last, reluctant screw. An interesting hum issued from within the hole, and there was an ugly dark spot on the outside of the loose plate where it had been scorched recently.

There was also a pretty glowing thing inside.

The alien couldn't read, either, so the characters etched into the swinging plate meant nothing to it beyond another smattering of red color. There was a lot of small print, and two big blotches of red, which spelled out:

CAUTION . . . LASER.

The Beachball took one bounce and stuck itself to the wall just outside the loose panel. It peered inward with whatever it used for eyes.

Two beams of intense red light flashed deeper into the dark interior, still steady, still in proper line. They issued from a complex instrument close by the portal.

If the Beachball had been at all familiar with starship construction, it would have noted instantly that the join between the light-emitting device and its base was no longer solid. Shifting its position on the wall, it reached in with both claws, touching, feeling, probing curiously for more tactile information about the thing that ended in the pretty lights.

The finely adjusted instrument moved slightly on its loosened mounting. There was a spark, a crackling flash. The Beachball honked in pain and jerked back out of the recess, bouncing at top speed out of the lock.

An occasional wisp of smoke came from the dark interior now, interspersed with odd electrical pops and crackles. It didn't seem very important.

Like everything else on the *Dark Star*, the appearances were deceptive . . .

They had twenty yards to go now for a first down—twenty yards to go because that schmuck Anderson had blown the last play totally and run into his own tight end.

Jesus, how could you run into your own tight end—even on an end around? But it had happened, and now they were back on their own ten instead of the twenty or maybe better, with twenty to go for a first and a third down and Coach had sent in Davis—that pansy Davis, the flanker—with the play and they were supposed to quick kick, fer crissake.

Quick kick with the third quarter almost over and them trailing and goddamnit that was no way to win football games.

Boiler pleaded and begged with O'Brien, the new quarterback. Just let them run another play. An off-tackle . . . a lousy off-tackle, geez! Fake the damn kick and have O'Brien take the snap and hand it to him and he'd follow Harris off the left side.

And O'Brien had hemmed and hawed and said what the hell, why not? He didn't like the coach and he didn't like kicking on third down and his girl friend wasn't putting out, so why the hell not?

The snap was made and Boiler yelled at Harris that if he didn't clear that hole for him he'd kick his teeth out after the game and the big black son-of-a-bitch just turned and smiled back at him and said don't worry, just follow me, man.

So they'd snapped and he'd seen it working right then . . . seen the stupid linebackers pull up close to try and block the kick and only two backs deep for the kick and O'Brien had stepped up and at the last second, perfect, took the ball instead of letting it go to Davis.

Tossed it to him like a volleyball, and he caught it and there was the whole left side of the line wiped out, just wiped out, man. And Harris out there running ahead of him. Old Mojack Harris, and the last linebacker recovering and trying to get over. Boiler laughed at the expression on his face as Harris wasted him. Put him on his can and then Boiler was running free, free, with the sounds of the crowd in his ears and the look on the coach's face turning from fury to cheers as he passed the first down marker and kept going.

A little sidestep here—the deep back never saw him and then it was nothing but grass, grass, man, all the way to the end zone, to those beautiful high-stickin' goal posts. And the cheering, oh man, the cheering as that crowd went absolutely nuts. Ninety yards off tackle, man. Ninety goddamn yards and the crowd so loud you couldn't hear yourself. Couldn't hear a thing, man, and the lights blinding you. Couldn't hear and couldn't see; couldn't hear and couldn't see, couldn't hear or see the alarm flashing on the screen behind him . . .

Talby blinked. He'd been star-dreaming again. It
seemed somebody was talking to him.

"So you see," Doolittle was telling him, glancing up
now and then from his seat in the little corner on the
other side of the open hatch, "so you see, sometimes
you'd get a wave that would just kind of fold over on itself. You know, like somebody whipping batter. And
you'd crouch down inside this tube of water, Talby, and
it would sound like, oh, like an express train coming up
right on your heels. Just like in a cartoon."

He glanced upward out through the dome, but the
blackness was beginning to get to him again. So he
stared at his feet. The sight was surprisingly comforting.

"You'd just crouch down on your board then, inside
that tube, and ride it and hope it never ended. If you
were a second too fast, you'd lose it altogether . . . be
out in front of it. A second too slow and the water
would just catch you up, swing you up and over and spit
you out somewhere high up on the beach. I tell you,
Talby, there's nothing like it. How does that sound to
you, hey, Talby? Talby?"

Talby was engrossed in watching words and numbers
form and realign on his tiny console screen.

. . . SYSTEMS STATUS POSSIBLE COMP 47308 . . .
MALFUNCTION POSSIBLE PRIMARY . . . SECONDARY
PRIORITY DEMAND . . . 1-2-3-4-5-6-7-8-9-10-MAX . . .
POTENTIAL CIRCUIT FAIL . . .

The last words vanished from the screen. It stayed
clear. That meant the ship's computer was working on
whatever the problem was.

A part of him—dim, social portion, vestigial appen-
dage—was listening to Doolittle say something about
water and a tube. He nodded politely at what he
thought might be an appropriate moment and was aware
of pleasing the lieutenant. The rest of him remained
fixed on the screen.

. . . RAD. REG 594 . . .

Now words and symbols and numbers began to flash
across the screen in rapid succession. They meant nothing and they meant everything, but it was one part of the

computer talking to another. It was too fast for even Talby to follow.

He relaxed again in the seat. The computer hadn't flashed any emergency buzzers, activated any warning lights. Whatever the difficulty was, the *Dark Star*'s brain appeared to have it under control.

He was aware that several emergency warning circuits had failed on and off for a number of years. This node of information was shunted conveniently aside. Right now he didn't feel like double-checking on the "emergency," if indeed there was one. Later, maybe . . .

A new star drifted slowly into view over the arm's-length horizon of the ship. His gaze locked on to it as efficiently as any tracking telescope. Definitely a new luminary to add to his growing personal catalog.

He set about logging it as enthusiastically as he had the thousands suddenly glimpsed on their first day out of hyperdrive.

Size, distance, possible planets, composition. More words were flashing across the screen now, slower, slow enough for human comprehension.

He was aware that these words meant something significant, but surely they could wait. There was nothing that couldn't be subordinated to the cataloging of a new star, for nothing was more important. Nothing!

Doolittle would have paid more attention to the words appearing on the astronomer's screen, but he was out of position to see it. And his mind was busy elsewhere, thinking of open, rolling sea.

Boiler would have paid more attention to the words, but his thoughts were on an open field.

Pinback was thinking of an open surface, period. Open surface of any kind, so long as it was solid beneath his feet, and equipped with the normal appurtenances—green grass, blue sky, a cloud or two, maybe even some real trees.

As for Commander Powell, his mind was just . . . open . . .

In addition to not paying attention to their communications screens, the crew members of the *Dark Star* were serenely ignoring what was happening beneath the ship. None of them heard the soft click inside the ship's largest chamber.

None of them saw the doors in the bottom of the ship slide back as they had numerous times before. A long magnetic grapple dropped down with a familiar oblong numbered shape attached to its base. Nor did they see the next series of words that flashed across every screen on ship.

. . . BOMB BAY SYSTEMS ACTIVATED . . .

There was a large 20 engraved on the side of this oblong shape. Thermostellar Triggering Device Number Twenty knew that it had been through this sequence before. It had a long memory capability programmed into a short life.

And it shouldn't have been through this before. It was programmed for this sequence only once, and here it was running through it a second time. The bomb searched those memory reels and found nothing to account for it.

Number Twenty was understandably confused.

"Ship's computer calling bomb Number Twenty. Ship's computer calling bomb Number Twenty. You are out of the bomb bay again. This is incorrect."

"I received the signal to prepare for drop again," the bomb replied with a twinge of electronic irritability.

Hesitation on the part of the *Dark Star's* brain. Recheck and correlate—ah yes, here was the difficulty.

"There is an additional unexpected malfunction in the laser system in communications which has not yet been rectified. This is the system failure which caused your former abortive drop. It apparently has not yet been fully compensated for. It has caused your drop system to pass an incorrect order again. I repeat. This is not a bomb run."

"All very plausible . . . but nevertheless, I received the drop signal."

"As stated, the signal was given in error."

"Oh, I don't want to hear that," the bomb muttered. A definite note of petulance had crept into its otherwise neutral tones. The longer the bomb conversed, the greater the danger of its fairly simple logic circuits growing confused.

"I order you to return to the bomb bay."

"Phooey."

The expletive was exceedingly mild, but the import behind it was not. The ship's computer considered what to do. Perhaps a more direct machine-to-machine approach was required.

"If you do not return to the bomb bay, you will be in direct contravention of Prime Ordinance One of Central Computer to Subordinate Computer relations."

"Sticks and stones will break my bones," the bomb started to reply.

"We have no time to discuss your internal configurations," the main computer countered. "However, I will elucidate at length if you will return to the bomb bay."

"Uh-uh."

"I ord—" the computer hesitated a microsecond, "I strongly suggest that you return to the bomb bay."

"That is counter to my current programming."

For the first time now the *Dark Star*'s brain revealed some emotion of its own—if indeed it is possible for a mechanical mind to indicate exasperation.

"Repeat. One of the communications-systems' lasers has sustained damage. The same accident also temporarily deactivated the tracer circuit necessary to locate the damage without manual aid. Until such aid is forthcoming I cannot rectify the damage, but it is certain that you received a false signal. Do you see this? You must return to the bomb bay while I identify the source of the false signal."

There was a long pause. Then the bomb agreed. Reluctantly.

"Oh, all right—but this is the last time."

Once more an internal hum sounded. Bomb Number Twenty obediently slid up on its grapple back into the belly of the *Dark Star*. The bay doors slid silently shut behind it.

6

TALBY HAD FINISHED cataloging his new star. There seemed to be a whole new grouping coming up just a few degrees north of their course, but he couldn't be sure yet. Best to wait a few minutes.

He could have made confirmation with the dome telescope, but that was for pleasure, for close-up peeks after the leg-work was done. Talby disdained using the scope. It was another way of degrading his work.

It would be a few minutes before the maybe-cluster hove near enough for dissection. His eyes strayed down to the viewscreen. Then the astronomer sat up a little straighter, forced his mind back down the parsecs.

What now showed on screen was a series of numbers, but they were as much his language as English. Rather more so, in fact.

"Doolittle, I have a malfunction indicated on this readout, but it doesn't say where it is."

"Glidin'," Doolittle murmured softly, his eyes glazed. "Glidin' down the long, smooth drop."

"Lieutenant Doolittle!" Talby said firmly.

Doolittle blinked. "Hmmm? Malfunction? Don't worry about it, Talby. Getting 'em all the time, now. We'll find out what's wrong when whatever is malfunctioning gets bad enough for the ship to complain—or when it stops."

That was quite true, Talby thought. Besides, he didn't care if yet another minor malfunction afflicted the ship. He used little enough of its rapidly diminishing creature comforts.

But if it was something that could interfere with the *Dark Star*'s operation, it might also be something which could interfere with his star-gazing, and that could not be permitted to go unchecked.

"I really think we should try and locate the source of the trouble right away, Lieutenant," he suggested. "It might be something vital—something affecting the ship's capability to perform properly."

"You know," Doolittle mused in a faraway tone, "I wish I had my board with me right now. Didn't have the sense to include it in my personal goods. They would have laughed at me, sure, but so what? Even though I can't ride it, I could always wax it now and then, and stand on it, and kinda wriggle my toes around on it. You don't know, Talby, the feeling you can get just standing on your board and thinking about the waves screaming in beneath you, screaming. . ."

Pinback was screaming. The elevator was moving up the shaft again. Just when he thought it might descend far enough for him to drop free, it clicked and started up.

Whatever random circuit was responsible for controlling its actions during this insane "test" appeared to be sending it up and down the shaft without rhyme or reason. There was no pattern to the jerky series of ups and downs.

There was the one normal doorway at the central level, but it was closed, of course, when the elevator was in operation. Every time they passed it, Pinback tried to swing his legs over far enough to give it a solid kick. Repeated contact might at least activate some emergency tell-tale up forward.

It didn't take him terribly long to override his embarrassment at being found like this. That was preferable to being found dead at the bottom of the shaft. Boiler would probably get a laugh out of that, too, he thought grimly.

It gave him more strength to hang on. He still had a pretty good grip on the bar, but he couldn't hang like this indefinitely. What were Boiler and Doolittle doing, anyway? Somebody ought to have missed him by now.

No, that was wishful thinking in the extreme. Privacy being the precious commodity it was on the *Dark Star*, no one would bother another unless there was work to be done that required his presence. Boiler and Doolittle might wonder at his absence, but they wouldn't think anything was wrong.

Eventually it looked like he was going to have to judge the elevator's lowest point of descent and drop free . . . and hope the impact wouldn't be too damaging. That still left him with the interesting problem of what to do if the elevator then decided to descent *all* the way. He might survive the drop in fine shape, only to be squashed flat at the bottom of the shaft.

That didn't seem likely, though. So far the elevator had shown no signs of dropping closer than twenty meters from the bottom.

But it was still too impressive a fall for Pinback to risk it, except as a last resort. He looked upward, examined the base of the lift. His gaze settled on a small plate just to the right center of the elevator floor. It seemed to protrude slightly from the rest of the metal.

Four simple wing nuts were all that held it in place. Of course—emergency access hatch!

Damning himself for being a complete idiot, he braced himself for the long reach. Then, hanging on with one arm, he swung free and batted awkwardly at the first nut A few twists and it was free. It clattered hollowly down the shaft.

He couldn't hang like that for very long. It took a moment of holding on with both arms before he felt strong enough to try again.

Tightening his arm, he swung over and worked at the second nut. It came free with gratifying speed.

The elevator was rising again. His left arm felt like an old section of tire. No way he could hang on much longer. He tried the third nut. It moved halfway down the screw—and stopped. He had to get back on the bar again.

He wasn't going to be able to do it. But the fourth nut flew off with a single swing of his hand. The plate was hanging loosely from one nut now. He let go, resolutely gripped the last obstacle, and turned it by hand once, twice . . . the nut came free, followed immediately by the plate, which clattered off his head and shoulder and almost knocked him loose.

A deep breath—he had just about enough strength left to try this once—and he swung free on his right arm. The other reached up and in, getting an unbreakable grip inside the elevator. A minute later and he had both arms inside—inside the warm, comforting, familiar elevator.

He was saved.

Pushing down on the floor, he brought his upper torso all the way in. He rested like that for a few seconds, catching his breath without fear of falling, and then pushed again—with no result.

His eyes widened slightly.

He was stuck.

He twisted and pushed, pushed and heaved, but either his arms were now so weak they couldn't force him through or, more likely, his hips were so fat that no amount of shoving and grunting was going to break him free.

No, he was securely trapped—unless, of course, he wanted to sneak his fingers between belly and gap and pull himself *down,* and start all over again.

Not much chance of that. Better stuck half in than falling whole. At least he was safe. He could relax and think his way out of this. Plenty of time, now.

Unless, he remembered again, the lift suddenly did

decide to descend all the way. He wouldn't fall, but he'd have both legs neatly pulverized. It might also break him free, but the odds were not inviting. He thought of having his legs slowly knuckled up beneath him, cracking like chopsticks, and he looked around wildly.

There ought to be—yes, there it was, a red phone receiver on the interior wall, over by the foredoorway. The receiver was set just this side of a control panel; and lower down than seemed reasonable. For once it looked like things had been planned with his troubles in mind.

Leaning until it felt like the metal floor was going to cut him in half, he strained to reach it. Strained, grunted, struggling for each millimeter.

The phone stayed just out of his reach.

Meanwhile, the elevator continued its Carrollian jaunts up and down the shaft. It had been terrifying to hang by his arms, expecting to go crashing to the bottom at any second. Now his body was safe and only his mind was shaky. Since he couldn't see below anymore, he had no way of knowing if he was within meters or millimeters of being crushed against the shaft floor.

Taking a deep breath and trying to get his internal organs on a vertical line, he somehow coaxed another centimeter or so out of the trap—just enough to fumble and knock the receiver off its latch. Breathing was difficult now.

But he had the phone. As he brought it near he thought once more of Doolittle and Boiler and their reaction when he buzzed them.

He could make up some kind of excuse. It shouldn't be necessary to let on that he had let the alien escape. Might not sound too logical but, by God, he'd make it work! Yes, he would be cool and reasonable and just properly aloof about it all, and they would accept his explanation.

That would come later. Right now he was still quivering in abject terror. There was the familiar click; he could feel the elevator descending and now visualized his legs as a mass of compound fractures. The "Help!" he screamed into the receiver was loud.

Unexpectedly, there came an immediate reply. But it was not the one Pinback was hoping for.

"I'm sorry," confessed a mechanical voice that was like but yet subtly different from the central computer's. "This phone is out of order. Please use an alternate ship phone until the damage has been repaired. Alternate ship phones are located at . . ."

Pinback's emotions rapidly ran the gamut from shock to hopelessness to outrage. Here he was trying to be the best member of the crew, and he found himself balked at every turn by sheer flight inefficiency. There was a conspiracy on this ship to hinder *his* efficiency.

Right now it was trying to render him not only inefficient, but inoperative.

He threw the phone receiver against the wall, watched it swing pendulumlike back and forth. "Please report the damage at once," the phone concluded.

Sure, he thought wildly. I'll just call it in through the nearest phone.

The control board! Fifty closely spaced buttons which would make the elevator do everything but return independently to Earth. They were set into the wall near the unmentionable receiver, but slightly farther away. That was one reason why he hadn't tried them first.

The other reason was that he could not remember what any button but number one did. Number one started and stopped the elevator. And strain as he might, there was no way he was going to be able to reach that farthest bit of plastic.

Now he wished he had taken the time to learn the function of the other forty-nine. Or had he? If he had, he couldn't remember them now.

Leaning toward the board, fighting at the constricting metal at his waist, aware that he might be only centimeters from smashing into the bottom of the shaft, he fought to reach the panel.

His finger fluttered over the ranked plastic, jabbed arbitrarily at one. Number forty-five. He felt it give under his finger.

There was a pause, then another voice began smoothly, "For your listening enjoyment, we now present excerpts from the *Barber of Seville,* by Gioacchino Rossini."

And a full-throated baritone promptly blasted from the speaker overhead as the elevator continued to descend. At least, Pinback thought it was descending. All motion seemed downward to him now.

Straining again, he punched in another button. No effect. Another, and another. He kept punching buttons until he achieved his second concrete result.

The baritone shut up.

More buttons, and then another recording.

"Good for you!" said the sprightly voice in a tone not unlike his mother's. "You've decided to clean the elevator. To clean and service the electromagnetic coils in the bottom, it is necessary to jettison the access plate in the floor. This may be done in slow or rapid sequence, depending on the required speed of cleaning."

Cursing silently, Pinback was starting to wonder why he had ever wanted to join the Advanced Expeditionary Corps. Something in the back of his mind tried to answer him, but it made no sense, none at all. He shut it off. This was no time for filling one's head with fog.

"To remove the floor plate for slow-sequence cleaning," the computer voice continued, "follow procedures indicated in Ship Service Manual SS-forty-six, sections E-thirteen through E-fifty-six."

"Great. I'll just whip out my ol' manual, here," Pinback muttered sarcastically.

"To remove the floor plate for rapid-sequence cleaning, press button number forty."

Well, that was more like it! Probably that would release the hidden catches and he could just lift himself completely inside.

He reached up, his hand flailing millimeters away from the indicated button. He grunted, twisted slightly.

C'mon, Pinback, just another couple of millimeters, boy, and you'll be safe out of this . . .

Finally he hit the button, let out a gasp of relief, and sagged back into the grip of the opening. But the relief failed to last.

Something was nagging at him. There was something he half recalled from a cursory restudy of the maintenance manuals. The electromagnetic bolts in the floor panel (electromagnetic bolts? What about the simple catches he'd been thnking of?) were normally released only once a year . . . slowly. He couldn't remember anything about rapid-sequence cleaning.

Only that there was some reason why it was rarely, if ever, done. Oh yes, that was it . . .

His eyes bulged.

"Attention, danger," said the computer voice sternly. "Attention, danger. Automatic charges will now activate the small explosive bolts in the plate unit for rapid-sequence cleaning, as slow sequence has not been initiated according to manual procedure directives. The plate will disengage for rapid cleaning in five seconds."

Pinback shook his head, screamed a silent *no!*, quite aware that verbalizing it wouldn't have any effect on the machine anyway. He shoved desperately at the floor plate, but he couldn't budge it. And it was a little late to be wishing he had spent more time in the exercise room.

Four glowing arrows had appeared in the bottom of the elevator, conveniently identifying the placement of the explosive bolts. Of course, the plate had to be used again, so the explosion couldn't be *too* powerful . . . could it?

He wished he could remember—and it didn't do much for his state of mind to see that all four arrows were pointing inward, toward him. It seemed somehow significant.

"Please leave the elevator immediately," the voice requested.

"I'm trying, I'm trying!"

"Five, four, three . . ." It occurred to Pinback, then,

that the . . . "two" . . . elevator was also out to . . .
"one" . . . get him . . .

Outside, in the main corridor of the *Dark Star,* a light
flashed on to indicate that the elevator was now opposite
the doorway. Little wisps of smoke, which, unlike the
light, were not regulation, began to drift from around its
corners. Then the double door slid apart.

Pinback staggered out. He was alive, even if he didn't
feel like it. His hair was a bit more rumpled than usual,
his clothing a mite more disheveled. Otherwise he was
basically the same, if one discounted the dark streaks
around his cheeks and neck and the slight scorched look
of his tunic around his waist.

A flood of acrid smoke poured out of the elevator behind him. Carbonized cloth, mostly, with a faint aroma
of Pinback to it. He had a neat black line under his
loose shirt where the severe jolt from the explosion had
thrown the metal even tighter against his belly.

Oh, and just above that was a neat square of metal—
the floor plate—still tightly wrapped around him.

He tried to slump into a corner, and failed. The plate
did not permit easy slumping. Or even sitting. And then
he had a very discouraging thought.

It occurred to him that despite all his precautions to
preserve his dignity—and nearly killing himself in the
bargain—his dilemma might have been revealed to
—Doolittle and Boiler anyway, if the explosion had set
any tell-tales in the control room or living area. He
watched the corridor ahead for long minutes. But no
one came down it to laugh at him, and he began to relax
a little. If the explosive bolts were part of a standard
maintenance sequence, and it was beginning to look that
way, then it shouldn't activate any special alarm anywhere elsc on board. Talby, Doolittle, and Boiler should
still be ignorant of the indignities he had suffered.

There remained the little matter of getting the plate
off. Another trip to the crafts room solved that quickly
enough. There was a small cutting-and-welding outfit
there—the psychometricians had thought of everything,
it seemed. It made a neat job of the plate, though a part

of him rebelled at the idea of slicing the bottom of the elevator into pieces. At the moment, though, his desire to be rid of the damn thing far outweighed any loyal considerations to preserve and protect the physical integrity of the ship.

Besides, if Boiler could blow holes in the cover to the heating unit for target practice, he could darn well play around with something that was even less integral to the *Dark Star's* operation. He could always fix the plate later, and for now there was still plenty of room to stand inside the lift.

But later, not now. Now he had something else to do. He smiled. Something *much* more important.

Once the plate was free, he made use of the small first-aid kit thoughtfully provided for clumsy craftsmen. That took care of his injured tummy.

Then he made his way purposefully back to the alien-holding room, checking the corridor ahead of him every now and then to make sure the Beachball wasn't waiting to playfully ambush him, and also to avoid Doolittle and Boiler.

As usual, the luminants rushed instantly to the close side of the cage, but this time they didn't make him nervous. He didn't bother to shoo them away.

They had no eyes, no ears, no recognizable features at all. Only perfect, regular, geometric shapes. Yet they always responded to his presence. He wondered momentarily what they thought, if they thought—what they felt, if they felt.

He knew what *he* felt.

The red box was labeled simply ANESTHETIC GUN. He started to break the seal, then paused thoughtfully and lifted the whole box neatly off its wall latch.

Better not load the thing until the last minute. If he ran into any of the others he couldn't claim he was going target shooting like Boiler. Not with this baby. Nor did he want to go walking around the ship with a loaded gun in hand. Not considering the predilection the Beachball had for dropping on to people without warning.

The way his luck had been running lately, he'd was likely to end up tranquilizing his foot.

But his luck, he told himself grimly, was about to take a forced change. He might have to hunt out the alien all over again, but chances were good that it was still hovering around the open shaft, perhaps waiting for the elevator to descend again. He hoped it was. There were too many hiding places in the rear compartments of the ship for him to search through without eventually coming to the attention of Boiler or Doolittle.

He encountered neither fellow crewman on his walk back to the chamber he had left so long ago. Only a few steps into it, he was brought up short by a familiar, now hateful, twittering sound.

He stopped, looked around slowly. Eventually his gaze went to the right and up, to rest on the alien. It was resting there, glued to the wall, the ugly red and yellow shape gobbling and honking softly at him as though nothing had happened.

Probably it wanted to play some more. Well, Pinback was through playing. Keeping a wary eye on the quivering Beachball, he opened the safety catches on the box and removed the pistol. He opened the chamber, reached in for one of the tranquilizer darts . . . and paused.

After all, bringing the alien aboard had been his idea. He had had to fight for it over the objections of the others, who had insisted that alien-gathering wasn't part of the *Dark Star*'s mission. But he'd persisted.

So in more than one way, the alien was his responsibility. He almost put the dart back. Almost. Then he grew determined and slipped the innocuous-looking little sliver of metal into the chamber.

Any feelings of concern he might have retained for the Beachball had been effectively negated by its several deliberate—yes, deliberate—attempts to kill him.

It made no difference to Pinback that the alien might have had nothing of the sort in mind, because it didn't have enough room in its mind for something like premeditation. He was going to be revenged—revenged for ev-

erything the unmentionable blob of sickening proto-
plasm had done to him. This time it was going back into
a cage for good.

Of course, there was one minor drawback in the use
of the emergency tranquilizer. He had no way of knowing whether it would even work on this particular example of otherlife. It might only make it mad.

Pinback checked to make sure the dart was seated in
the chamber of the compressed-air pistol and that the
air charge was up to power. The dose might also prove
fatal. There was only one way to find out.

The alternative was simply to blast it to organic powder with the laser, but Pinback's fury hadn't gone quite
that far yet. Better to give it some sort of chance.

Besides, he was afraid of the laser.

Snapping the chamber closed and raising his arm
carefully, he took aim at the oscillating spheroid.

"Now it's time to go sleepy-bye, you worthless piece
of garbage."

He pulled the trigger. A short puff from the gun and
the dart struck square in the center of the alien.

There was an unexpected loud whooshing sound, and
the alien shot violently toward him. Pinback ducked
frantically, raising his arms to ward off the seemingly
vicious charge. Then he straightened uncertainly, aware
that the alien had missed him by several meters.

It continued to roar around the room, accompanied
by the whooshing sound of escaping gas, bouncing haphazardly off walls and ceiling. Its speed was beginning to
decrease rapidly, and the whooshing noise decreased to
a faintly obscene snicker. It came to an exhausted stop
in a far corner.

Pinback stared at it askance, then walked over. He
bent over it and touched it. There was no repetition of
the burning sensation he had received when he had tried
to get the rubber mouse away from it.

He felt the limp object. There was a solid lump
around the bottom, consisting of the clawed feet and
contracted internal organs. But when he picked it up it

hung wrinkled and sagging in one hand. It was, indisputably, dead.

Geez, he muttered to himself. His anger was now as deflated as the alien. He hadn't really wanted to kill it. Just to knock it out and get it back in its cage.

Now it was pretty pitiful-looking, all collapsed in on itself, like a jellyfish washed up on a beach. Geez, he whispered again.

The worst part of it was, now they would never know how intelligent it might have been, because the specialists back at Earth Base would never have a chance to run their tests on it—and he'd never get his medal.

Nor would it look very good in the official reports. Not that Doolittle or Talby or Boiler would care. It wasn't part of their mission, as Doolittle had insisted. Boiler would probably find the sad state of the dead Beachball hilarious, after his own perverted fashion.

But it definitely wouldn't look good in the report. He could visualize the entry now:

"Sergeant Pinback, in attempting to recapture one of the alien specimens—which he inadvertently allowed to escape—overdosed it with tranquilizer."

Aw, nuts . . . dosage had nothing to do with it. It was the deadly hypodermic point that had done the damage. How was he to know that the alien would be so thin-skinned? He was no xenobiologist.

Besides, he could forgive a lot of things, but not that time when the alien had taken the broom away from him and beaten him to the floor with it. That was the last straw.

He pulled the tranquilizer dart out of the now-rough skin and examined it with new respect. It was a good thing the first shot had struck home. He could see the alien imitating this action, too, grabbing the missed dart and jabbing it into Pinback. He grinned slightly. That would have looked a damn sight worse in the reports.

"Sergeant Pinback, in attempting to recapture one of the alien specimens, was tranquilized by said speciman and placed in a cage."

Why was he berating himself, then? The alien had

brought this on itself. Hadn't it nearly killed him in the elevator shaft? Why was he always tearing himself down?

He'd just done a good—no, a brave thing, going back in after a semi-intelligent alien that had nearly killed him. Yeah, Doolittle would be proud of him, and even Boiler might sit up and treat him with a little more respect.

He started back toward the alien-holding chamber with the dead Beachball in tow. Even so, he didn't think he would mention this little episode to his fellows right away. No sense overawing them with his inordinate courage too soon. He'd slip them the information in small doses.

As for the alien, the arts-and-crafts room was equipped for just about every hobby, and he'd never taken a crack at half of them.

Taxidermy, for example . . .

Boiler was checking out some jury-rigged repairs they had made on the electronic head. It had been damaged when their original living quarters had blown, and now there were subtle hints that it was not recycling their waste products properly.

Since everything on the *Dark Star* was recycled and reused, including all their food and drink, it was vital that this particular piece of equipment work properly.

Slipping his hand deep into the open wall panel, he felt around until he located the slot between the two pressure-activated reconstituters. Gently, he hunted for any hint of a loose connection.

Not all of the crew's "special" pictures decorated one wall in their temporary living quarters. There were a number of the finest on the walls in here. They provided a pleasing backdrop to his current activities.

He found himself thinking more and more often of women lately, despite all the preconditioning the psychometricians had laid on him—despite all the advanced autoerotic devices included on the *Dark Star*. He found himself seeing round shapes and curves where there should have been only sharp corners and flat sides. Found himself actually feeling warmth and blood where there was only plastic and indifferent current.

Found himself thinking of the party . . . that incredible party after they had won the conference championship. Found himself thinking of the last week on Earth, the final week before they entered solitary preparation for the mission, and of Diane . . . especially of Diane.

Tall, quiet, compliant, insecure, affectionate, indifferent Diane.

Wherever she was now, he wished her well.

None of the connections were loose. Maybe the monitors on the tubing linkup . . .

Everything had worked out so fine, so nice, so *natural,* to the point where he had even stopped thinking of going on the mission. They could replace him easily enough.

That beautiful, deep brunette . . . and then she'd gone back to "the older guy," the one she had "no serious relationship with." Just up and disappeared out of his life.

That made it easy for him to score high on the tests, easy to devote himself to becoming part of the *Dark Star* itself. He hadn't thought anything but cold, technological thoughts for a long time.

But lately . . . women. And especially a certain woman. Occasionally a part of him would stir with a violent internal tremor and cry, *Diane, Diane!*

"Easy." A hand came down gentle, firm on his shoulder and his head snapped around, upward. "Easy, Boiler." Doolittle said it softly.

Boiler let his emotions simmer, quiet, evaporate. Then he eased his hand carefully out of the slot, began tightening the bolts on the panel.

"I can't find anything wrong with the reconstituters, Lieutenant. And the tubing connections seem firm."

"It's all right, Boiler. It's all right. Maybe it'll clear up. There might just be some accumulated blockage in the system. Let's go get something corrosive to eat and see if we can't clear it out."

Boiler looked up at him and then smiled ever so slightly—as much as he ever smiled. Both Talby and Pinback were certifiably nuts, but what about Doolittle? He couldn't figure the lieutenant out. What did Doolittle think about behind that Assyrian beard and Egyptian stare? What was he thinking about now, looking down at Boiler and not really seeing him?

Were they really on this last bomb run, the last run before they could start the long, lonely journey back to Earth? Or on some journey less profound and more internal—like Boiler's own?

He shook his head once and tightened the last bolt. Leaving the driver carelessly on the floor, he followed Doolittle up the near ladder.

His thoughts shrank to a tiny ball and normal emotions replaced personal ones as Pinback joined them.

"Hey, guys. Guys?" Pinback began brightly. "You know the alien? The Beachball? Well, it attacked me, guys! Twice, and I tried to tranquilize it but I ended up killing it. But not because of the tranquilizer. That's the interesting thing about it, you know?"

Doolittle led them through the door to the combination galley and dining room.

"Hey, yeah, this is a good idea, Lieutenant," he blabbered. "I'm kinda hungry, too. Well, anyhow, I shot it with the tranquilizer gun and it just spewed out gas like crazy and shot around the room like a punctured balloon. I guess its insides were mostly just that, plain old gas. It was just filled with gas."

This information was not met with a barrage of questions on the part of Doolittle and Boiler.

"Hey, guys, how could it live and just be filled with gas?"

"I wonder what we got to eat today?" Boiler grumbled.

"I thought I was gonna die. I was hanging to the bottom of the damned elevator for twenty minutes."

"Probably chicken again," Doolittle theorized. He had long suspected that the menu for the *Dark Star* had been planned by more than one colonel.

"I probably saved the ship," Pinback continued excitedly. "Why, that thing might've . . ."

The kitchen–dining area was not very big. The men were not required to eat their meals there; it was merely suggested, since the area was equipped with powerful suction devices and cleansers that gleaned every drop of spilled food for reconstituting.

There were a couple of seats and three blank walls facing a fourth. That wall contained machinery as complex as anything on the bridge or up in the astronomer's dome. Concentrated food was prepared here, waste products finally recycled into new food and drink.

". . . could have done some real damage!" Pinback finished.

Boiler was down now, really down, after his internal outburst of a few moments ago. "God, I'm really sick of chicken."

It was beginning to dawn on Pinback that his account of an overwhelming victory over the rampaging forces of alien malignancy were generating something less than an ecstatic response on the part of his audience. He folded his arms and retreated into the inevitable pout.

"Well, if that's the way you feel about it, then I just won't talk about it anymore."

"Hey, that sounds like a fine idea, Pinback," Doolittle observed. He moved to the service oven and punched the DINNER call switch three times in measured succession. There was a click, a quiet whirr that lasted for several seconds, and then the door slid aside.

Doolittle peered in, wrinkling his nose as he got a whiff of the heated liquids inside.

"Chicken," he muttered. He thumbed another switch and the door closed. Once more he activated the call button thrice. Another buzz, another whirr, a different smell.

"Ah, ham." Either the machine had finally learned to read their discontent or else they had simply gotten a break. Why so much chicken had been programmed into their diet was beyond Doolittle's imagining.

Actually, the only difference between the "chicken"

and "ham"—or steak, seafood, or meat loaf they were offered—was in the artificial flavoring, since they were constantly consuming the same basic series of protein-carbohydrate-sugar solids. And since all the liquid concentrates looked the same, the psyche boys no doubt concluded that taste variety was important.

Why, then, this unnatural preponderance of processed fowl? Doolittle suspected that, like everything else on the *Dark Star*, there was a kink in the kitchen computer too. But that was one piece of instrumentation he didn't want to chance fooling with. Not as long as it kept them alive.

Attempts at reprogramming the flavoring in their food might result in even worse offerings. They might get oyster stew for a month, something that had happened several years ago. Doolittle had nearly starved. He did not like the taste of oyster stew, or the look of oyster stew, or the smell of oyster stew.

Unquestionably, Doolittle was afflicted with an anti-oyster bias rooted deep in childhood neuroses.

That didn't increase his fondness for chicken, however.

Thirty years of schooling come to this, he mused. A superbly trained technician and here he was, his mind reduced to debating the demerits of chickens and oysters. God, the workings of a technological society!

Talby was the only one who didn't care. To Talby, food was so much fuel, something that distracted him from his primary task of observing the universe. Something to be gotten over with as fast as possible. A necessary if irritating activity, like going to the john or sleeping.

Juggling the three packages because of the heat, he removed them from the oven and handed one each to Boiler and Pinback.

"Dinner, fellows."

"Chicken again?" Pinback asked, staring doubtfully down at his package.

"Almost, but no—ham for a change."

"Oh . . . good."

So much for pre-dinner conversation. They began peeling the foil from the tops of the metal containers. Each tray-shape held four transparent plastic packages of concentrated liquid food.

Doolittle tried to open his own without looking at the contents. A man could lose all his teeth in space—through calcium loss, say—and still survive in excellent health, thanks to this diet. But you wanted something to sink your teeth into after a while. They had experienced no calcium loss and had perfect artificial gravity. Therefore Doolittle felt he had a reasonable complaint. There was no reason why the corps could not have provided them with some real food.

But the astronauts had all asked that before, and the reply was always the same: It was wasteful. Crumbs always got lost. Bones were sheer space-takers, as were skin and fat and gristle—except in proper liquid portions. On the other hand, the concentrated liquids were neat, there was virtually no waste except for occasional spilled drops—and even these were recoverable—and they could be rapidly and easily recycled. Furthermore, they were exceedingly simple to prepare.

All of which Doolittle recognized and none of which he agreed with. Had there actually been a time when he had felt that the overflavored concentrates tasted good? Or had that, too, been another lie to get him on the mission?

Now more than ever he regretted the explosion which had cost them Boiler's supply of real food. "Swiss cheese and knockwurst and thick gooey peanut butter," Boiler had said, and more. Doolittle suddenly, surprisingly, found his mouth watering.

That was it—think about Boiler's lost cache while slurping down this oily mess. Think about rye bread and onion rolls, and hot corned beef with mustard.

He tore the corner off one of the plastic tubes, dropped it in the proper recycling receptacle (inorganic), and began sucking at the liquified vegetable inside.

The thoughts seemed to help a little . . . split pea soup and crab gumbo and turkey gravy . . . though he would have traded his next week's rations for a single thick, greasy salami.

"Hey, Doolittle." Pinback was sucking on a tube of blue fluid.

"Yeah?"

"Think we'll ever find any *real* intelligent life out there? I mean, the Beachball had something, but it wasn't real intelligence." At least I don't think it was . . . I hope it wasn't, he thought silently.

"Out where?" Doolittle didn't look up.

"Oh, you know . . . where we're heading now. The Veil Nebula region."

The frustration and boredom and reality of twenty long years in empty space found expression in Doolittle's terse reply. If someone back at Earth Base had told him he would have felt this way, been capable of voicing such words at any time during the mission, Doolittle would have laughed at him.

But the sentiment came easily now, with a casual bitterness he barely noted.

"Who cares . . . ?"

7

Talby stepped carefully down the ladder and headed purposefully toward the seldom-used corridor deep in the center of the *Dark Star*. The green glow of the lights set in the walls and ceiling marked the way to the central computer.

He could have gone forward to the control room–bridge and used the annex there, but he wanted to check out something on the main computer itself. Besides, the central computer room was actually closer to the dome than the bridge. And he didn't see the need to alarm the others. Besides, they were enjoying their dinners now. No point in disturbing them unless the problem turned out to require their help. He was uncomfortable down here. Odd how nervous he became these days, away from the friendly stars. There had been a time when he'd felt perfectly at home within the ship. A long time ago.

"Back, Talby," the heavens whispered. *"Come back."*

"It's just for a couple of minutes, that's all," he murmured to himself. "Only a couple of minutes. But if there's a possibility of a serious malfunction, then I have to check it out. You understand that, don't you?"

"Come back, Talby . . ."

"I have to . . . because I don't think Doolittle or the others will. They don't care anymore."

"Back, Talby," a red giant whispered, a titanic voice roaring in his brain. *"Back to us, Talby,"* replied a mild sun not unlike old Sol.

A ghostly quartet moaned at him with a combined voice like rising wind over a lake—a remarkable quaternary system of four stars circling about one another.

He *had* to check out the indicated malfunction. A switch, and the double-shielded door slid aside.

"Hey," said Pinback, pausing in the middle of a tube of dessert, "did I ever tell you guys how I got on this mission? Did I ever tell you?"

Doolittle indicated the tiny bottle on the table, and Boiler passed it to him. It consisted of auxiliary flavoring, and the meals computer changed its contents daily. He tried it in one tube. Vanilla today—interesting, even with the potatoes.

"Yes, you did, Pinback," he replied.

But the sergeant was off, and nothing short of catastrophe could stop him.

"It's very strange, you know, how it happened, but—"

Boiler groaned softly. "There he goes again."

"Don't get excited, Boiler," Doolittle advised. "It won't do any good and it won't shut him up. He's got to finish."

Boiler turned away.

"I wasn't an astronaut to begin with, see."

Wait a minute—what was he saying? Of course he had been an astronaut! Then Pinback smiled inside. Might as well get the crazy story out. It was only a dream, of course. Just a weird dream that had been repeating itself over the years. It seemed very real, but naturally most dreams did.

Still, it was peculiar that he should find himself repeating so many times. At least it was amusing. And he seemed to be having it less and less now.

"See, to qualify for astronaut rating, you had to score

at least seven hundred on the Officer's Corps SARE's,"
he explained. "And I made fifty-eight . . . but I wanted
to stay in the program. So they put me into liquid-fuel
maintenance on the launch pad, working with the boosters for the starship.

"The boosters were liquid fueled, of course, since the
Dark Star couldn't use its overdrive field within the
Earth's gravitational influence. It was an important job
and—"

Boiler glared back at him, but this time it failed to in-
timidate Pinback, just as Doolittle had indicated.

"Ah, naturally I was . . ." Pinback was aware of
Boiler's unpleasant scrutiny and strove not to look at
him, ". . . ah, really disappointed. I wanted to be an astronaut in the worst way, and I don't think those tests
ever really measure your capability . . ."

"He told us this," Boiler mused while Pinback ram-
bled on, "four years ago last, didn't he?"

"I mean, you know, I'd always had this urge to help
push back the frontiers of space, get habitable systems
ready for the colony ships. Anyway, I was on duty on
the pad when they were getting ready to launch the ship
. . . the *Dark Star.*"

Doolittle sipped at the last of his dinner. "No, I think
it was four years ago."

". . . I was checking out the fuel lines on the big KG
tanks at the time . . ."

"That's what I said," a puzzled Boiler commented.
Doolittle looked over at him and frowned slightly.

". . . And this astronaut came running out from behind the crew-isolation shed. He was stark naked, and
he had his starsuit in one hand and, well, I evaluated the
situation and immediately surmised that he was insane.

"He threw his starsuit on the ground. Then he saw
me and gave me this really funny look, you know, and
then I was *sure* he was insane, which really bothered
me, because those guys are supposed to be about the
stablest people there are. Then he opened the lid on the
KG tank and jumped in." Pinback's tone turned earnest.
"He was holding his nose, but I was sure that wouldn't

make much difference, guys, because as you probably know, liquid KG is kept at about minus two hundred and twenty degrees Centigrade and is pretty corrosive stuff besides.

"Well, I was pretty surprised, I can tell you. I didn't know what to make of it. Like I said, astronauts are supposed to be super stable, and here this guy comes running along stark naked and jumps into my KG tank."

"Can I have some of that?" Boiler pointed to an unopened packet still resting in Doolittle's tray.

Doolittle nodded and hand d the corporal the plastic container. He didn't care much for liquid rolls and butter.

"Well, naturally," Pinback continued relentlessly, "I was gonna try and save him . . . even though by that time, what with the super cold and corrosiveness and all, there probably wasn't much left of him . . . but I mean, what's a guy gonna do? I couldn't just stand around and do nothing, could I?"

He shrugged ff the nagging feeling that he shouldn't be saying all this, that he'd gone through this insane dream too many times already. The feeling stayed with him, but he continued.

"So I put on his starsuit for protection, and I'm getting ready to go in after him . . . right, you guys? So what happened was that before I could leap into the vat . . ."

Doolittle gave him a sad look.

". . . this other fella came running along. He took a fast look at the name on the starsuit and says, 'Hey, Sergeant Pinback, you've gotta board immediately because we're gonna launch in twenty minutes.' "

Doolittle's patience was just about exhausted. "You told us this four years ago."

"And I tried to tell him," Pinback continued, ignoring the lieutenant's comment, "that I wasn't really astronaut Sergeant Pinback."

What was that? Hold on there . . . you gone bananas or something, Pinback? Of course you're Sergeant Pinback. Who else could you be but Sergeant Pinback?

". . . but I couldn't figure out how to make the helmet radio work . . ."

"It's funny, you know," Boiler said, trying hard to remember exactly and rubbing his chin, "but I'm sure it was four years ago."

"Maybe," Doolittle admitted. It was beginning to bother him now. At first he had shrugged off these trivial lapses of memory. After all, in twenty years it was hardly reasonable to expect that you'd be able to recall every tiny little thing that happened.

But the lapses seemed to be increasing. And he wasn't alone in forgetting things. Boiler, too, was having trouble with the same memories—memories of things not directly connected with the operation of the ship. Pinback, poor Pinback, had problems of his own, as did Talby.

Doolittle could remember everything about his personal life before starting the mission, and everything necessary to the *Dark Star*'s operation—but anything in between gave him increasing trouble. It was beginning to be as if he had had no personal life at all in the past twenty years. As though nothing had happened not involving the mission.

As though his mind now as well as his body was becoming an extension of the ship. A voice screamed inside him.

One more bomb! One more drop, and they could start home.

But would they get there in time . . . ?

Talby was seated before the computer keyboard. He blended neatly into the machinery. The main computer screen faced him, illuminated from within, framed by the green glow of the computer-chamber lighting.

At the moment the screen was flashing an ultrarapid series of mathematical symbols and words for Talby's perusal. As usual, he had better luck following the symbols than the words.

It gave him some idea of where to look for the trouble. The computer's own tracing circuits had apparently been damaged. That accounted for its failure to locate and announce the trouble. It needed help—Talby's.

Repunching orders via the keyboard, he called up a chart of the *Dark Star*. More buttons pushed, more detailed graphs appeared.

He was clearly going to have to pinpoint the problem himself. More requests were fed into the ship's electronic ganglion. The area of the ship under consideration was patiently reduced as one section after another checked out clean.

Finally an intermittent red flash appeared on the screen, accusing the rearmost section of the ship's schematics.

He immediately punched out a request for that area, then saw it appear obediently on screen. The red flash was still there. He punched for an enlargement of the damaged area. It expanded tremendously. A final enlargement, and the bright red warning light turned into a winking arrow jabbing at a back section of the emergency airlock. And at last, words appeared underneath the diagram.

COMMUNICATIONS LASER NO. 17—EMERGENCY AIRLOCK

Talby's thoughts moved one step ahead of the series of repair-and-realignment orders that followed. He thumbed the intercom switch to one side without even looking at it and spoke toward the mike.

"Lieutenant Doolittle, this is Talby. Please reply, Lieutenant, wherever you are."

"I'm here, Talby," came Doolittle's voice. "What is it?"

The astronomer considered his words carefully. He had to impress the importance of the situation on Doolittle without nenecessarily alarming him. He didn't want the lieutenant to send Boiler or Pinback back to help him—they made him nervous. He was pretty sure he could handle it alone, without having to look at another human being.

"I'm sorry to interrupt your evening meal, sir, but I'm in the computer room. I've located the malfunction."

"Malfunction? What malfunction?"

"You remember, sir. The one that the computer couldn't locate. You were in the dome with me when it came in."

"Oh . . . sure," Doolittle replied in a tone that hinted he was anything but.

"The scanner shows it to be a breakdown in the number seventeen communications leaser, down in the emergency airlock. I can't tell exactly what's wrong with the laser, except that it has something to do with alignment. That could be dangerous, but since nothing disastrous has happened since the malfunction first occurred, I tend to think it's okay . . . I'm going to put on a starsuit in a little while just in case, and go back and see if I can't fix the trouble."

"Sure, sounds good, Talby."

"Just wanted to let you know, Lieutenant."

"Yeah, fine. Doolittle out." He slipped the mike back under the playback grid.

Now what had Talby been talking about? Some sort of malfunction? Well, it didn't matter. If it were really important, he would see that Doolittle knew about it.

"Why doesn't Talby ever eat down here with the rest of us?" Boiler asked.

Doolittle looked over at the corporal, surprised. It wasn't like Boiler to show concern for anyone. He shrugged. "He just likes it up in the dome, that's all. You know . . . astronomers."

As if that were the final word on the subject, both he and Boiler became quiet. Doolittle finished off the last of the packet of ham and went to his final drops of mint tea. That was the best thing about the food computer, as far as he was concerned, and the best parts of their meals. With no effort, the computer could produce packets of any tea known to man—Darjeeling to Lipton. Sometimes the new flavors were all that kept Doolittle going.

If Doolittle had his teas, Boiler had his reconstituted cigars. Now he reached into a tunic pocket and extracted one of the long smokes. Pity their reconstructed food didn't taste as good as the cigars smoked.

Lighting up, he took a couple of long, satisfied puffs. His brow wrinkled at a sudden thought.

"Hey, Talby—Talby who?" His confusion deepened, but he didn't let it get to him. You couldn't let anything get to you now or you were sure to go off the deep end. "What's Talby's first name?"

Doolittle looked up casually, started to say something, and suddenly appeared absorbed in an entirely different thought. A mild hint of worry crept into his voice.

"Hey, Boiler . . . what's *my* first name?"

Boiler opened his mouth to reply, hesitated, closed it.

"So anyway," Pinback went on as if they had been entranced by his reminiscences all along, "after they discovered the bits and pieces of this . . ."

Doolittle got up and dropped the remnants of plastic and metal into the proper disposal slot.

"I'm going to the music room."

"So anyway," Pinback began again, shifting to face Boiler.

Boiler didn't even look at him, didn't even say anything. He simply rose and tossed his used utensils into the same slot and left the eating area.

And Pinback—Pinback was mad. Here he'd just saved the whole damn ship and no one was the least bit interested in how he had come to be aboard to do it. But if that were the case, then he hadn't been talking about saving the ship, had he? He'd been talking about saving someone else. An astronaut, yeah, like himself. Or was it? He wasn't sure.

Getting up, he properly disposed of his own garbage and thoughtfully pressed the recycle button—something Doolittle and Boiler, typically, had neglected to do.

There was a hum from the disposal as he left the room, thinking hard. Saved. Astronaut. Himself, Pinback. Alien. Tranquilizer. Beachball.

He was definitely confused and worried, and at times when he was confused and worried there was only one way he could find solace.

Each of them had their own place. Boiler could do it anywhere, with occasional bursts of barely controlled

violence. Doolittle did it in the music room. Talby did it
. . . Boiler's last words came back to him and he suddenly wondered what the hell Talby's first name *was,*
anyway.

As usual, the recording alcove in the library was un-
occupied, but he took the precaution of checking the
corridor before he closed the door and sat down. Privacy was essential here. It wouldn't do for Boiler, or even
Doolittle, to see what he was up to.

He removed the precious, unmarked tape from his
shirt. The legend *My Diary* was scrawled across the otherwise blank label. Gently he slipped it into the machine
and turned his attention to the screen in front of the
compact console.

A muted hum indicated that the audio was activated,
and then the words FOR OFFICIAL PURPOSES, THIS RE-
CORDING INSTRUMENT AUTOMATICALLY DELETES ALL
OFFENSIVE LANGUAGE AND/OR GESTURES appeared on
the screen.

There was a last pop, indicating that the visual was
focused and in synch with the sound, and then the words
disappeared. They were replaced by a portrait of a
young man, staring back at him. A stranger.

The stranger looked very much like himself. The dif-
ferences were quite superficial. The stranger was neatly
clad in a finely pressed uniform. His hair was closely
trimmed on top and sides and the burgeoning beard
carefully shaped. He wore a silly smile and a generally
immature expression.

Beep. "This statement's for posterity," the stranger
declaimed vigorously. Pinback sat perfectly motionless,
watching him.

"I just wanna say that I am not Sergeant Pinback. My
real name is Bill Frug. Frug. F-R-U-G. I'm a field maintenance technician. Specifically, I work with the KG liquid fuel tanks for the starship launch pad chemical
boosters.

"I've been on this mission now for about fourteen

years, Earth time. Or about . . ." he paused a moment
to figure, ". . . two years shiptime.

"That's a long time, two years shiptime. Fourteen
years I've been on this mission and I just wanna tell you
that Pinback's uniforms do not fit me, and the under-
wear is too loose, and I've been trying to make up my
own nametag to replace Sergeant Pinback's, but I can't
seem to get his nametags off any of these jumpsuits
without ripping the suit and besides, the sewing machine
in the recreation room doesn't work anymore, and I
only know how to do hemstitching anyway.

"I do not belong on this mission, though so far I have
been . . . an exemplary member of the crew and have
tried to fulfill Sergeant Pinback's duties to the best of
my ability and . . . and . . . I want to go home."

The picture changed. The stranger still looked like
Pinback, only now his hair and beard were longer, much
longer, and so was his expression.

"Ah, Commander Powell died today," the stranger
intoned solemnly. "We were coming out of hyperdrive
after a successful bomb run and, well, he sits right next
to me and, well, something went wrong with the force-
field mechanism when we came out into normal space
and it triggered a defective circuit in his seat and it blew
up and—"

The figure on the screen gave a half-shrug, "—and he
was dead, just like that. Doolittle said his brain was still
functioning, sort of, so instead of giving him a burial in
space we put him into the freezer in the hopes that when
we get back to Earth, the bio boys can reconstruct a
body for him.

"Personally, I think Doolittle is unduly optimistic, but
then he always was kind of close to the commander and
so I understand his actions."

Yet again the video metamorphosis, and an even
more disheveled Pinback-type stared forlornly out at
Pinback.

"Doolittle says that he's assuming formal command of
the ship," the figure said, "and I, I say . . ." The word

DELETED momentarily replaced the figure on the screen, and the audio went silent.

". . . that he's exceeding his authority because I'm the only one with any objectivity left on this ship and therefore I should be the one to assume command. Doolittle says that I'm not really Sergeant Pinback, which shows how far gone he is, and so I couldn't possibly assume command.

"Then he said that if I wanted to take over he would be perfectly happy to let me. And he asked what my first order was and that stupid ape Boiler just stood there and snickered at me and I didn't think it was very funny. Or fair. I mean, I should have some time to prepare for something like taking command.

"Now, I'm filing an official report on this to Earth Base headquarters 'cause I think this is a lot of . . ." and the word DELETED appeared again—several times, in fact.

The view changed again. Now it was a smiling, happy Pinback-type who appeared, with slightly trimmed beard and hair. A Pinback who looked very much, if not exactly, like the Pinback sitting in the recorder chair, staring at his mirror image on the screen.

This time the audio came only in uneven bursts, with the now familiar slogan DELETED appearing almost constantly on the screen. Very few real sounds escaped the recorder's inbuilt censors, and these were mostly snickers and nervous half-giggles instead of words.

"I went up to Doolittle in the hall today," the image giggled, "and I DELETED Doolittle." Snicker. "He said DELETED" . . . grin, chuckle, snort . . . "and he didn't . . ." This time the words GESTURE DELETED appeared. "Then he," . . . laugh, DELETED, chuckle . . . "and I said, well, and he *still* didn't get it, and . . ."

The beep changed the screen yet again, to reveal now a nervous, irritated Pinback who in addition to looking very unhappy also revealed a slight twitch at the corner of the right eye.

"This mission has fallen apart since Commander Powell died. Doolittle treats me like an idiot. Talby, he thinks he's so smart, up in his dome, and Boiler punches me in the arm when no one is looking.

"I'm tired of being treated like an old washrag. I'm tired of being treated like I'm an intruder and don't belong. I'm tired of not being given due credit for the job I'm doing. I'm tired of . . . of not being treated like I should be treated.

"After all, I outrank both Talby and Boiler, and I've reported their disrespect back to headquarters. But for some reason headquarters hasn't responded. I wonder what's wrong with those people down there. Don't they realize the importance of maintaining discipline up here? If rank means nothing anymore then we might as well give up on the whole mission. It's enough to make someone resign his commission.

"I would relinquish my post and duties except that my sense of loyalty to the program runs too high. Besides, it would endanger everyone on the ship, myself included. If this is selfish self-preservation, then so be it."

That was the last speech. The tape froze and the information AWAITING TAPING flashed on the screen.

Pinback let out a deep sigh. He adjusted his tunic slightly, smoothed back some free-flying hairs, and brushed a little congealed liquid ham out of his beard. Sitting up straight and clearing his throat, he flicked another switch on the console and spoke toward the machine, staring straight ahead. His tone was even, well modulated, controlled—maybe a touch overcontrolled.

"I do not like the men on this spaceship. They are uncouth and fail to appreciate my better qualities. I have something of value to contribute to this mission, if they would only take a little of their so-precious time to recognize it.

"Today, over lunch, I attempted to improve morale and build a sense of camaraderie among the men by holding a humorous round-robin discussion of the early days of the mission. My overtures were brutally rejected.

"These men do not want a happy ship. They are

deeply sick and try to compensate for their own mental misfortunes by making me feel miserable."

He was dimly aware that he was sniffling and that this was wrong. Also unmilitary. It should not be going on the tape. But he couldn't stop himself, and besides, it felt good. The words continued to flow.

"Last week was my birthday. Not only didn't I get any presents but nobody even said 'happy birthday' to me. And there was no cake, either. When I asked about it Boiler suggested I go stick my head in the reactor core and blow myself out."

He sniffled again.

"Someday this tape will be played, and then they'll be sorry."

That seemed to be everything. Anyhow, he was sniffling too hard to make much sense, and there was no point in clogging up the tape with too much emotion, however honest or heartfelt. It wasn't dignified.

Reaching out, he flipped down the activate switch and the Pinback on the screen disappeared. Pinback carefully removed the tape from the recorder and slipped it back into his tunic. Then he got up and headed for the sleeping area.

There were a few hours left in overdrive before they reached the target planet. Sitting down on his bunk, he methodically turned off the intercom, warning controls, everything. He didn't want to be disturbed. He still had some time to sulk, and he didn't want Doolittle, or Boiler, breaking in on him.

So he didn't hear it. And Doolittle, deep into his makeshift organ, didn't hear it either, because he turned off everything when he was playing. Everything except the plink and bang and clonk of crude hammers striking water jars and old metal containers and the rank on rank of huge pipes blasting out the Franck *Grande Pièce Symphonique*.

And Boiler, deep, deep in his fading girlie magazine, didn't hear it either, not with the earmuffs on. Didn't hear the insistent voice of the computer . . .

8

"ATTENTION, ATTENTION, ALL personnel. I have finally identified the malfunction." This would have been of some import to Talby, but he was asleep. He shouldn't have been, but no one could dictate sleep periods to Talby any longer. Besides, there would always be someone else awake if he chose to dose off at an odd moment.

They were awake, all right, but they weren't listening.

"Communications laser number seventeen has been damaged," the voice continued. "This damage was apparently incurred during the passage through the electromagnetic energy vortex we recently encountered.

"As you will note, this laser monitors the jettison primer on the bomb-drop mechanism. Communications laser number seventeen is located in the emergency airlock. It is crucial to attend to this malfunction before engaging primer for the next bomb-run sequence. Thank you for observing all safety precautions."

And Boiler slept on innocently under his girlie mag and Pinback was asleep under his thoughts and Doolittle played on and on and on and Talby lay asleep thinking about tomorrow's stars . . .

Talby was musing on his new sky. Waking up in the

dome was the usual exhilarating experience. A beautiful morning.

What a joke that was. He hadn't seen a morning in twenty years, except for the false tint of a sun coming up over a soon-to-be-destroyed unstable world. Morning, indeed.

And he had another job to do, as necessary as it was distasteful. That of repairing the broken communications laser. Still, it shouldn't be too hard to fix.

As usual, he was awake before any of the others. After a quick check to make sure all ship's systems were operating more or less normally, he made his way to the emergency airlock. No point in waking Doolittle. Be easier to tell him about the successful completion of the repair job from the comfort of the dome.

The four suits were untouched, neatly ranked side by side in the open locker. The sooner he got this job over with, the better.

He probably didn't need the starsuit. But if for some reason the laser should backfire, the suit was just reflective enough to deflect the beam away. It wouldn't stand up to a direct blast from the laser for even seconds, but there was no point in taking any more chances than he had to.

While he busied himself with preparations, Doolittle, Boiler, and Pinback had already risen and dressed. It was Doolittle who aborted breakfast. A quick check forward revealed that they were about to come within drop range of the target world. Pinback argued for breakfast —the planet wasn't going anywhere, and they had a couple hundred thousand years before it grew dangerous.

But there was no restraining Doolittle. This was the last planet, the last run, the last bomb. Boiler didn't care about that so much, but he was always ready to destroy. Eating could wait.

They moved forward, slipped into their respective seats, and began checking out instrumentation. Suddenly they were a team again, a tripartate, animate machine, all personalities forgotten.

Boiler activated the overhead screens.

"There she is." The planet that occupied most of the telescopic finder was deep red in color, showing a surface seething with titanic volcanoes higher than three or four Everests. Spewing, vomiting the insides of the globe outward, collapsing into glowing canyons many miles in depth—an unstable world if ever they had encountered one.

"Ninety-nine-percent-plus probability," reported Boiler, checking his gauges, "that this world will deviate from its normal orbit within another twelve thousand rotations. It'll spiral in toward its sun and—"

"Eventual nova," finished Pinback.

"And this system has a perfectly good Earth-type world." He gestured at the red monster glittering on their screens. "Sounds good. Let's vaporize it."

Operating in perfect unison, the three men set timing devices, adjusted minute controls, prepared the *Dark Star* for the drop to come—a unified force operating to produce a momentary orgy of destruction.

An orgy of which this was to be the final, conclusive orgasm, and then . . . home.

Pinback was the first, by a split second, to lean back in his seat. "Bomb-bay systems operational."

There was a familiar hum from deep in the bowels of the ship, and once more the white coffin labeled "20" slid smoothly out of the ventral hatch. Doolittle donned his headset, leaned forward, and worked his console.

"Lock fail-safe."

Pinback plugged in the dual jump for the required connection overhead, smiling as he did so. Doolittle, Boiler, Pinback: the names meant nothing now. How significant . . . but he had no time to think about it.

That's why he liked these climactic runs. They gave him no time to think. He hit the double switch.

"Fail-safe in lock."

"We have," Boiler announced, "eight minutes until drop. Twenty-four minutes until detonation. All systems are go and functioning."

Words and symbols alternated on separate screens in their confirmation.

"Sidereal time at sunlight velocity," Pinback confirmed. "Destruction sequence status initiated." There was a clearing of the screens and then the multiple zeros at the base all changed to twenty-four. Seconds began to tick away.

He sighed, leaned back in his seat—squirming uncomfortably for a moment, as he always did. Sure, Doolittle and Boiler could laugh, but Powell had been sitting next to *him* when they'd come out of hyperdrive and his seat circuit had blown. Powell's blank eyes had been staring *him* in the face.

Why wouldn't they understand back at Earth Base, and send him replacement circuitry?

No time for this now, Pinback. You are On Duty.

He flicked the pi kup that was set into his headset, heard the echo signifying operational status.

"This is Sergeant Pinback calling bomb number twenty. Sergeant Pinback calling bomb number twenty. Do you read me, bomb?"

"Bomb number twenty to Sergeant Pinback. I read you, Sergeant."

"How's it going, bomb?"

"All systems are functioning perfectly, Sergeant Pinback. Everything is going well."

He'd heard the same answers many times before. Why, he wondered idly, couldn't they at least give the bombs different voices? The answer occurred to him as soon as the thought was completed.

It wouldn't do to give a suicidal machine a distinct personality. Not that it would make any difference to the bomb, which was barely conscious of itself as an individual organism, but Pinback could imagine that it might begin to get to the crew.

Why, if you weren't careful you might start to think of the mechanical thermostellar triggering devices as people, people you were sending to an inevitable fate, people who had no chance to develop their really fine minds, people who . . .

Easy, Pinback. That's a no-no. Better think the right thoughts or they'll take away your teddy bear.

Elsewhere on the ship a different computer voice was reciting information to a suit-enclosed Talby.

"You are now in the emergency airlock. Please remember that in an emergency situation the surface door can be opened instantly without the need of prior depressurization. So be sure to wear your starsuit at all times. Thank you for observing all safety precautions."

Talby ignored the message. He knew the regulations by heart and didn't need to be reminded of them by a solicitous machine. All he wanted to do was finish this repair job and get back to his dome and stars.

He was already searching the room before the recorded message concluded. The emergency airlock wasn't terribly big, so it didn't take him long to locate the open slot over the communications laser where the protective panel had dropped away.

Even though there was no reason for the mirrors in the laser to be activated, he was cautious as he bent to inspect the interior. A laser was something like a tornado; you could pass within millimeters of the crucial area without being hurt, but cross the ultimate line and you got burned.

In addition to the scorched panel, he saw that the laser itself had been knocked slightly out of alignment. The mounting was loose. Well, that ought to be easy enough to correct. It would be a ticklish bit of work with the laser in operation, but there was nothing complicated or time-consuming about it.

He gave a little smile of satisfaction. This job wouldn't take more than a few minutes of careful work with a screwdriver. Even if the mounting was broken he could easily readjust the angle of the beam to compensate.

Placing the little toolbox he'd brought along on the floor, he hunted inside for the driver with the proper head, then spoke into his helmet mike.

"Lieutenant Doolittle, sir . . . Talby here."

Doolittle heard him, but he was monitoring drop instrumentation, for crissake, and had no time for Talby's philosophical drivelings.

"Sssh, Talby," he muttered absently into his own pickup. "We're in the middle of a very complicated maneuver. Don't bother me now."

"I think this is important, sir," the astronomer insisted. He was inspecting the interior of the laser housing again. "I think I've located the malfunction the computer announced. You remember, sir. I'm in the emergency airlock now, and—"

"Not now, Talby!" Doolittle said irritably. Damn the man! Spent all of his time isolated in his little dome, not even sharing a meal with his buddies . . . hell, not even sleeping with them, and he just wanted Doolittle to drop everything to listen to his personal problems.

"Well, I'm in the airlock, so I'm going to go ahead and—"

Thoroughly annoyed, Doolittle shut off his channel. Talby wouldn't talk to him when he, Doolittle, needed somebody to talk to, so by God, he wasn't going to sit here in the middle of a run—the *last* run—and exchange pleasantries with him.

He had a planet to destroy.

Odd how normal the ultramelodramatic phrase had come to sound. It was true—people could get used to anything. Repetition made playing God seem commonplace.

"Four minutes to drop, bomb," Pinback was saying conversationally. He seemed to get along well with the bomb brains—better, in fact, than he did with either Doolittle or Boiler Maybe it was because he had more in common with them. For example, there were plenty of times when he wished he could self-destruct, too.

"Have you checked your platinum-iridium energy shielding? That's important, you know. We must remember to check our energy shielding."

"Geezus," muttered Boiler, appalled at Pinback's attitude toward a metallic *thing,* as usual. And as usual, Pinback ignored him. Boiler couldn't talk to the bombs.

Even Doolittle had trouble sometimes. It was the one area in which Pinback excelled.

"Energy shielding positive function," the bomb replied happily.

Pinback yawned. "Remember your detonation time?"

"Detonation in twenty minutes."

"All right," concurred Pinback. "That checks out here. Okay, bomb, arm yourself."

Below the *Dark Star* there was a brief flash of lights on the bomb's casing, after which it said calmly, "Armed."

"Hello, Lieutenant Doolittle," Talby repeated into his suit mike. "Hello, hello, can you read me? Boiler, Pinback—do you read me on the bridge?"

Damn, now what? Another malfunction, or was it just that Doolittle didn't realize what he was doing back here? Didn't he understand that Talby'd found the damage and was going to repair it?

Well, it probably didn't make any difference. They were obviously busy with something forward. At least he wouldn't be disturbed with silly suggestions. He started to lean into the open slot . . .

"Communications laser number seventeen," the computer voice announced sharply, "monitoring the bomb-drop mechanism has now been activated and will switch into a drop mode. If you will look near the surface panel, you will see that the tell-tale light is on, thus indicating that the parallax receptive cell has been engaged."

Tell-tale light . . . the surface panel had been knocked off. Talby pulled his head quickly out of the housing, screamed to himself in confusion.

What the hell did Doolittle think he was doing? Was that what their "complicated maneuver" was all about? They couldn't run a bomb drop with a busted monitoring laser! Not only could something unimaginable go wrong with the drop, Talby could get himself punctured.

He stood there indecisively, debating whether to go ahead with the seconds-long repair or run forward to tell the others. But if it were only a couple of minutes to drop—a short run—he might not make it in time.

While he remained paralyzed, the computer voice continued. "The laser will now energize. Please stand clear of the path of the beam in the event that the protective panel should fail."

What panel? . . . the panel was off, you stupid . . . He took a hurried step backward.

"Communications laser number seventeen is now on test."

There was a dull but distinct crack and two parallel beams of pure red light leaped across the emergency airlock just in front of Talby. They drilled a pair of neat holes in the far wall of the lock, but apparently cut through nothing serious. They were high-intensity, short-focus beams and wouldn't go so far as to hull the ship, but some damage had already been done.

Worse might happen if he failed to repair the malfunction before the bomb was dropped.

He had already activated the darkening element in the starsuit helmet, so he could look at the beam without suffering retinal damage.

"Under no circumstances," the computer continued, "remove the panel and enter the path of the double beam. Thank you for observing all safety precautions."

"They're actually going through with a bomb run," Talby muttered. What was wrong with Doolittle? Had the lieutenant gone mad, like Pinback and Boiler?

"Doolittle . . . Lieutenant Doolittle, acknowledge. This is Talby. Emergency call . . . anybody on the bridge, acknowledge . . ."

Doolittle, Pinback, and Boiler—the anybodies—relaxed in their seats, each submerged in his own pre-drop thoughts. All ran their own obstacle course of emotions prior to a drop.

Boiler thought about the destruction on an unprecedented scale which they were about to commit, and smiled. Pinback didn't even consider that they were about to obliterate a whole planet, remove an entire world from the scheme of things; his concern was for the poor, unthought-of bomb.

Doolittle always went back to a book he had once read, an old book about the dropping of the first thermonuclear device on a city in . . . Japan, wasn't it? Went back to the thoughts of the pilot after seeing what he had wrought.

Of course, this was considerably different, since no lives were involved. And the worlds they smote were unstable, a threat to the lives of future colonizers. But he couldn't escape the nagging feeling that on any of the planets they had destroyed, despite careful pre-surveying, there might have been an indetectable, intelligent race to whom that world was home.

A race whose collective murder he bore on his conscience.

Ridiculous, absurd—instruments carefully checked each candidate for oblivion before they made their drop. But the thought persisted, mingled with those of that long-dead bomber pilot, and troubled him . . .

Pinback glanced at the chronometer and spoke into his headset pickup. "Everything looks fine, bomb. Dropping you off in about seventy-five seconds. Good luck."

"Thanks," came the mild reply from bomb number twenty.

Boiler was checking his readouts. "I get a quantum reading of thirty-five over thirty-five."

"I read the same here," agreed Doolittle.

If they didn't abort the run—and there seemed no reason to assume they would—he *had* to adjust the laser. Talby closed the toolkit and spoke into the pickup at the same time.

"Doolittle . . . Doolittle. I don't know if you can hear me, but I'm going to try and adjust the mounting under the laser to realign the beams properly. If you can hear me, hold off on the run till I finish. It won't take long."

Staying as much to the left side of the opening as he could, he balanced the driver in his right hand and controlled the haft of it with his left. Thus carefully balanced part in and part out of the alcove, he slid the driver toward the mounting.

He hit the proper screw on the first try and smiled to himself. It would all be over with in a minute.

Turning the driver slowly, he heard the click-click of the screw mechanism as the mounting tightened up, saw the laser housing start to shift on its base. Another couple of turns and he'd be through.

As the mounting shifted, it contacted a tiny printed circuit that had also been edged ever so slightly out of place. The circuit shorted, the current fed back into something it shouldn't have, and the something exploded.

The laser wheeled crazily on its mount, the beams shifted, and the darkened face plate of the astronomer caught the full brilliance of the twin beams.

Talby staggered backward, dropping the driver and grabbing for his eyes and clutching only the smooth glass of his helmet.

"My God . . . I can't see!"

Something was calling insistently behind the pain. "Attention, attention. The monitoring laser has malfunctioned. Under no circumstances . . ."

"Oh my eyes . . . I can't see, I can't . . ."

". . . enter the path of the beams. To do so will cause the instrumentation to immediately . . ."

Staggering blindly about the airlock, Talby fell into the twin lines of crimson. A violent concussion shook the airlock. The ravening feedback traveled back up numerous electronic neurons all the way into the central computer itself.

Circuits shorted in the hundreds, fluid-state controls shattered. Small fires broke out in the central computer, were immediately snuffed out as automatic fail-safes isolated the injured sections, amputated the outraged portions of the badly damaged network.

The tell-tale lights on bomb number twenty flashed a second time. They flashed normally—and unexpectedly, because the primary drop sequence had already been engaged. There was no reason for them to flash again.

The single flare of light at the magnetic grapple was *not* normal.

On the bridge, however, all was quiet, all was as it should be.

"Begin final drop sequence," said Pinback. The three men worked easily at their consoles. Then Pinback, after checking with his fellows, reached out and grasped the two switches which would do the thing.

"Marking . . . ten, nine, eight, seven, six, five, four, three, two, one . . . drop," and he turned both switches simultaneously to release the bomb.

He was rewarded instead with a brash, utterly alien honking that had all three of them looking wildly about the bridge.

Boiler finally spotted a couple of flashing red gauges, gauges he had never had occasion to observe in operation before. Pinback, meanwhile, had completely lost his aura of command and relaxation, exchanged it for one of more normal hypernervousness.

He looked around hopelessly, assuming that the end of their private universe was at hand. But neither Doolittle nor Boiler, though obviously worried, had panicked yet. He got a hold of himself and sat up straighter in his seat. They'd been too busy to notice his embarrassing reaction.

He waited for somebody to tell him what to do.

"Negative drop," Doolittle finally said, confirming what all the instruments told them. Tiny knots were pulling tighter and tighter inside him.

"Try it again, Pinback. It's just sitting in the bomb bay."

All three reset their controls, readjusted all switches for a repeat of previous actions.

Pinback counted again, from ten, to five, four, three, two, one . . . drop. Turned the dual switches only to hear the violent honking resume.

"Negative drop," Doolittle said again, no longer quite as calm of voice.

The bridge became a flurry of activity. Circuitry was checked and rechecked. Monitors were asked to produce explanations, yet insisted nothing was wrong. Gauges were studied for reasons overlooked; they stared back with blank glass faces and told nothing. As far as their instruments were concerned, the bomb had dropped and the crew of the *Dark Star* had gone off the deep end.

"Visual confirmation," suggested Boiler. "Maybe its the non-drop pickup that's malfunctioning."

Doolittle flipped the necessary lever. The chronometer, still ticking away the seconds, vanished from his screen and was replaced by a camera-view of the bottom of the *Dark Star*.

A long white box occupied much of the picture, resting serenely just below the open bay doors.

One glimpse was more than enough for Doolittle. He switched back to the chronometer, which now assumed a previously unheld importance. Overriding importance.

"It's there, all right." He thought rapidly. "Never mind the magnetic grapple. This is the last run. Let's blow the attachments." Boiler and Pinback nodded— Boiler once, curtly, Pinback hard enough to shake his hair.

"Rechannel all safety relays," the corporal said. "Open quantum latches."

"Open circuit fail-safes," Pinback put in.

"Cancel thrust-drive fail-safes," Doolittle added.

"Automatic valves open?" asked Pinback.

Boiler: "Check valves open . . . all connections severed . . . all explosive bolt fail-safes removed."

"And prepare for manual drop," Doolittle muttered grimly, "and . . . re-mark."

"Resetting," Pinback said quietly while both Doolittle and Boiler watched him. "Mark it . . . five, four, three, two, one, drop." He turned the switches and the honking came. That loud, abrasive, hysterical honking.

It sounded damnably like a laugh. They were laughing at him again, Pinback thought emotionally. He wrenched at the switches, staring at the screen above, trying to stop the laughing.

First it was Boiler laughing at him and punching him

in the arm when no one was looking and Doolittle had
been terse and abrupt with him the whole trip and Talby
up in the dome when he wasn't staring at his idiot universe was probably laughing at him too and now, now
the ship itself was laughing at him, at poor, stupid Bill
Frug Pinback Frug Bill . . .

"Drop!" he screamed at the flashing red warning
lights. "Drop, drop, drop!"

"Easy, Pinback," Doolittle said softly. "Take it easy,
man."

Pinback looked wildly over at him, panting hard.
Then he stared back down at the two switches he had
nearly pulled out of the board.

"He'll be okay, I think," Doolittle said in response to
Boiler's glance. "How about the bomb?"

"It's just sittin' there," the corporal told him, turning
his attention back to the readouts. "The damned thing's
just sittin' there. What the hell's wrong?"

And while they sat and wondered and fumed, above
each man a series of numbers set into a box insert at the
bottom of his screen, read: SIDEREAL BASE TIME
0014:40.6 DESTRUCTION SEQUENCE IN PROGRESS.

The number changed even as he looked at it, changed
while the honking sounded warningly throughout the
bridge. It resounded in the bomb bay and in the badly
damaged computer room and in the emergency airlock,
where an unconscious Talby lay sprawled beneath twin
lines of red, hands clasped over his face plate in a frozen
attempt to reach his eyes.

"Boiler," Doolittle said finally, nodding in the direction of the blaring speaker, "kill that thing."

Boiler reached out and flipped a switch on the small
panel marked *Audio*. The honking stopped. The red
warning light stopped with it, but the chronometer insert
in the screen did not, nor did the official one set into the
main console. All continued to tick off the seconds,
splitting the shrinking time period into tiny, manageable
bits and pieces.

"Oh, come on, Doolittle," a voice inside admonished
himself. "Don't just sit there on your ass. *Do* something,

man, or the bomb'll do it for you. The bomb is stuck in the bomb bay and it's primed to go off in about fourteen minutes and if it does, baby, the shock wave you'll be riding won't come from that wave breaking tight behind you."

He fumbled at his headset, spoke haltingly. "This is Lieutenant Doolittle calling bomb number twenty. Acknowledge, bomb number twenty."

"I'm here, Lieutenant."

"Sounds sane enough," Boiler observed.

"Computer, this is Doolittle. Talk to the bomb and order it back to the bay, please."

Silence.

"Computer, acknowledge. This is Lieutenant Doolittle speaking."

Quiet.

"You talk to it, Doolittle," suggested Boiler.

Doolittle nodded, cleared his throat. "There has been a malfunction again, bomb. You're to disarm yourself and return to the bomb bay immediately. There has been a malfunction. This bomb run is aborted. Return to the bomb bay immediately. Do you understand?"

"Yes." The bomb's voice was calm, composed. "I am programmed to detonate in fourteen minutes thirty seconds. Detonation will occur at the programmed time."

Frantic thoughts ran through Doolittle's mind. They were unencumbered by solutions. And on top of the bomb, he now had another problem to worry about.

What was the matter with the central computer?

"Bomb," he finally managed to sputter into the pickup, "this is *Doolittle*. You are *not* to detonate. I repeat, you are *not* to detonate in the bomb bay. Disarm yourself. This is an order. Do you read me, bomb?"

"I read you, Lieutenant Doolittle," the bomb replied quietly. "Locale of detonation is not a concern of mine. That is always predetermined . . . and I will detonate in fourteen minutes. Detonation will occur at the programmed time."

"You already said that," Doolittle said tightly. The bomb did not venture to argue this point.

"Fourteen minutes to detonation," Pinback informed them with a touch of desperation. "What the hell's happening, Lieutenant? What's going on?"

"I don't know." He spread his hands helplessly. "I can't figure out what—"

"Attention attention," came a familiar feminine voice —a voice Doolittle had not expected to hear again. He stopped in mid-sentence.

"I have sustained serious damage," the computer told them. "All fires in the region of the main computer room are now under control."

"Fires?" exclaimed Pinback, twisting in his seat. "What fires?"

"Shut up," Boiler whispered warningly. Pinback shut up.

"Please pay close attention. Bomb number twenty has not malfunctioned. I repeat, bomb number twenty has not malfunctioned. The failure to drop on command stems from a compound malfunction of communication laser number seventeen, which primes and follows through all drop orders via the release mechanism in the grapple shaft.

"All contact with the grapple shaft—and therefore with the bomb itself—is now cut off.

"I have subsequently activated automatic dampers on board ship. With no planetary material to react with, this damping will confine the thermostellar trigger reaction to an annihilation area approximately one kilometer in diameter. This is all I can do at this time.

"I am attempting to circumvent the damaged circuitry to reestablish contact with the grapple shaft and the bomb. I must inform you that prognosis for eventual success is not good. Repeat, not good. Damage *can* eventually be repaired, with manual human assistance, in twenty-four hours.

"All estimates indicate that even with human assistants operating under drug-stimulated efficiency, these repairs cannot be duplicated in fourteen minutes. It's all up to you now, fellows."

There was a moment's silence while the three crewmen digested this information. Boiler's voice was unnaturally subdued.

"Did you hear that, Doolittle?"

"Yeah, Doolittle," Pinback added pleadingly. "What are we gonna do? I mean, it's great that the automatic dampers will confine the explosion to an area only one kilometer in diameter, but if we and the ship are included in that kilometer, it's not gonna make a whole helluva lot of difference."

"Don't just sit there and stare, Lieutenant," Boiler said anxiously. "Give us some orders. What do we do?"

Why me? Why did he have to be the only officer left aboard when Powell died? Why couldn't he have been a simple underclassman like Boiler, or an indifferent loner like Talby, or even a posturing imposter like Pinback? Poor, well-meaning Pinback. Poor, ulcerous Boiler. Poor, distant Talby.

Poor Doolittle.

"I don't know," he said finally, honestly. "I don't know what we're going to do."

And Pinback said, almost predictably, "Commander Powell would have known what to do."

"Pinback," Doolittle said quietly, "if you say that one more time—if you even whisper it under your breath and I hear you—I'm going to kill you."

Pinback sat back in his chair and crossed his arms indifferently. "Won't make any difference. We're all gonna be dead in"—he squinted upward—"thirteen minutes twenty-five and a half seconds, anyway." He sniffled. "Commander Powell would alrcady have—"

"That's it!" Doolittle screamed.

Pinback gave a little jump and cowered in his seat, but Doolittle wasn't heading for him. Instead, he looked almost relieved.

"That's the only thing left to do. I'll have to ask Commander Powell. I'll have to ask him what to do." Doolittle was unstrapping himself from the chair.

"I don't mean to be a downer, Lieutenant," Boiler put in, "but Commander Powell's dead. He's been dead for a long time now. We put him—"

"His body's dead, yes," admitted Doolittle, "but we've kept him iced and wired. We got to him right after the accident. You know I've been able to get through to him a couple of times since."

Boiler was shaking his head disparagingly. "Freak shots . . . chance. There've been lots of times I've tried to talk to him and I get nothing but static . . . background noises from a half-dead mind."

"I tell you, he's not completely gone," Doolittle insisted. "Only his body is dead. If we can get him back to Earth before the cells degenerate too far—"

"If we can get ourselves back to Earth," Pinback mumbled.

"I'm going to try it anyway," he told them. He left the bridge, hurried through the corridors of the *Dark Star*.

Powell . . . Powell would know what do. Powell had always known what to do. Powell wasn't much older than the rest of them. Not physically. But he'd always seemed to know exactly the thing to do, always known the right decision to make.

It seemed to Doolittle that he relied more on Powell dead than when the commander had been alive.

If only that damned seat circuit hadn't gone bad on them. But there might still be a chance. He *had* talked with Powell since the accident—with what was left of him. There might still be a chance. With the central computer helpless, there *had* to be a chance.

He opened a secondary hatch, descended a ladder to a little-visited section of the ship. He remembered the trouble they'd had installing the linkups to Powell's brain. Remembered the pressure of that first attempt at contact.

How dimly, almost imperceptibly, Powell had responded to his first hesitant probes. It had given Doolittle something else to do after he'd finished the organ. Powell had become something of a hobby.

But he hadn't been down here in a long, long time. How badly had the leads disintegrated? How much had the supercold affected the linkages?

Carefully avoiding the thick hatch cover in the center

of the small chamber, whose top gave off continuous wisps of chilled air, he took the special insulated gloves from their place on the wall.

Then he walked around behind the hatch and lifted it carefully, slowly. The cover to the cryogenic freezer compartment came up easily. He could feel the cold even through the thick hatch insulation, even through the specially treated gloves.

Doolittle let the hatch cover down easily, took the linkup box from its niche in the wall. He plugged it into the open socket by the hatch cover and pulled out the compact mike. Adjusting dials on the box carefully, he watched an arrow move back and forth in a gauge.

Occasionally a hum like the ocean heard inside a seashell would rise to audibility, then die out. Eventually it reached a point where he could hear it clearly, where the arrow locked into the proper slot on the gauge. He turned another switch, and the arrow stayed frozen in position. If he couldn't reach Powell now he'd never be able to.

One other thing was certain. He'd never have another chance.

Below him, encased in frozen gas and ice of unbelievably low temperature, was Commander Powell. The body of the maybe-dead commander was nude, his head facing the hatch opening, his feet the farthest away.

The top of his skull was an intertwined blackbird's nest of long hair and wires and jumps and pickups and electrode paste. Both Boiler and Pinback had laughed at him for leaving Powell's hair unshorn—would have made it much easier to connect the myriad links. But Doolittle had insisted on leaving the commander as natural-looking as possible.

Actually he'd been as shocked as any of them when that first successful contact had been made. But Powell really had very little to say, and the conversations obviously tired him, drained what little was left of the life force.

So Doolittle had gone down to the cryo chamber less and less. And there had been many times when patient inquiry had drawn nothing but a confused mumbling from the commander's frozen brain.

But now—now he had to make contact.

He blew into his gloves and spoke hopefully into the box-microphone.

"Commander Powell, Commander Powell, this is Doolittle. Can you hear me, sir?"

Mumbling, becoming slightly louder, but still indistinct. He wasn't getting through. Wishing he had more delicate controls, he worked at the single fine tuner on the box.

"Commander Powell, this is Doolittle. Something serious has come up, sir. I'm sorry to bother you, but I do have to ask you a question. It's vital, sir. I know how this tires you, but I didn't know what else to do."

A slight turn of the tuner . . . and now words started to form, the mumbling started to take on recognizable form. The words were incomparably distant, faint . . . and cold. Cold with a chill born of vast distance and not the refrigerating material in which the commander was encased.

There was a feebleness to the words that Doolittle tried hard to ignore, and again he found himself speculating on what Powell's preserved mind thought about down there in the cold and the dark. He shivered a little. Maybe his desperate attempts to preserve the commander's life had not been a good thing.

But it might save them all, now.

This time, Powell seemed actually happy for the company.

"Doolittle . . . I'm so glad you've come to talk to me, Doolittle. It's been so long since anyone has come to talk to me."

"Yes, sir, Commander," he answered hurriedly. This was no place for long pauses—he had to retain Powell's attention. It could fade at any time.

"Sir, we have a big problem, and everything I've tried has failed. The computer is damaged and it can't seem to do anything, either. It's the last bomb, sir, bomb number twenty. It's stuck. It won't drop out of the bomb bay, and it refuses to abort, and it says it's going to detonate in"—he checked his wrist chronometer—"in less than eleven minutes . . . Do you understand me, sir?" His voice rose nervously. Had he lost the commander already?

Powell's voice echoed from the box speaker, reassuringly strong. "Yes, Doolittle . . . I hear you. Doolittle, you must tell me one thing."

"What's that, sir? Anything . . ."

"Tell me, Doolittle," came the distant, icy whisper, "how are the Dodgers doing?"

For a moment Doolittle sat frozen himself, trying to readjust his mind. "The . . . Dodgers?"

"Yes, Doolittle, the Dodgers. Do they have a chance for the pennant this year?"

Careful, now. His mind is wandering. Keep him happy, but keep him!

"They broke up, I think, sir. Disbanded over fifteen years ago. The descendants of the original landowners finally won their suit and they had the stadium torn down. I think they grow grapes there now."

"Oh," the ghost-voice moaned in disappointment. "Pity, pity. You see, Doolittle, all is transitory, nothing lasts. You realize that in here. It is surprising, but being dead has its advantages."

"Yes, sir—but you don't seem to understand." He had the tiny microphone in a strangle grip. "It's the bomb. We can't get bomb number twenty to drop. It's stuck in the bomb bay, we can't seem to abort the final sequence, and it insists it's going to detonate."

"Yes, Doolittle. But you must remember one thing."

"What, sir?"

"It's not a bomb. It's a thermostellar triggering device. There is a difference, you know."

If he doesn't start talking about the bomb, Doolittle thought tightly, I'm going to kill him.

"Whatever you choose to call it, sir, it's still going to go off. It'll kill us all."

"That's really not much concern of mine, Doolittle." A vast sigh rolled out of the mike. "But I can see where it might bother you." Another sigh. "So many malfunctions. Sometimes I wonder if—"

The voice stopped, then continued even more strongly. "Why don't you ever have anything nice to tell me when you come to visit me?"

"I'm sorry, sir," Doolittle said in a carefully controlled tone. "It's hard to think of nice things to say . . . even if you do have a nice disposition for a dead man. But you know, sir, so many malfuntions, and me with the responsibility of running the ship . . . Boiler is a walking bomb, and Pinback is receding into infantilism in addition to his special problem, and Talby grows further away from us every day. It's been very hard for me, sir." He checked his wrist chronometer. "But we're managing, sir. But the bomb . . ."

"Oh, yes. Ah, well . . . did you try the aesthemic clutch?"

"Yes, sir," he responded gratefully. At last Powell appeared to recognize the problem!

"What was that, Doolittle?"

"Negative effect, sir."

"It didn't work?" Powell moaned.

"That's what I meant by negative effect, sir."

"Don't get smart, Doolittle." A far-off, faintly heard wind. "What about the explosive bolts?"

"No luck, sir," Doolittle told the box.

"Tch. Well then, what about the aesthemic clutch?"

Doolittle wanted to scream. "You already asked me about that, sir, and I told you it didn't work either."

Rushing-water sounds of a distant, lonely creek. "Sorry, Doolittle. I've forgotten so much since I've been in here. So much . . . and I don't seem able to remember things in any order. I can remember some very complicated things, though, Doolittle, but I forget the simple ones, and I remember simple ones but forget the complicated ones, and forget the simple . . ."

"Sir? What should we *do,* sir? Time is running out. The bomb's going to go off in a few minutes!"

"Well, what you might try if everything else has failed

is to—" A roar of static took over the mike and Doolittle worked frantically to reset the controls.

"Commander?" He shook the box in deperation. Please let him finish, he pleaded with unknowable deities—please! "Hello . . . come in, Commander Powell!"

"Hello, Doolittle."

"Sorry, sir." Doolittle's turn to sigh. "You faded out for a couple of minutes there."

"I'm sorry, Doolittle. It's hard to keep in touch. Tiring. It makes you sleepy. So . . . sleepy . . ."

"The bomb, sir? What were you saying about the bomb—about what we might try?"

"Oh, yes, I remember, Doolittle. Did you think my mind was going? It seems to me . . . sorry, I've drawn a blank. Can't seem to remember . . ."

Doolittle was going to cry.

"Hold it, hold it. I'll have it again in just a minute. I forget so many things. Hold on just a second . . . let me think. Oh yes, now I remember . . ."

Tell me, tell me! "Yes, sir, what is it?"

"You might try to reach station KAAY in Los Angeles with an extreme tight beam, using your full amplification on the communications transmitter. They should know how the Dodgers are doing."

He covered the pickup with one hand and allowed himself the luxury of a single scream.

He'd have to start all over again.

"But you *can't* explode in the bomb bay," Pinback explained for the hundredth time. He stole a fast look at the chronometer insert in the screen overhead. It now showed 0009:08.1. It seemed like the numbers were changing faster now, but of course that was only his imagination working faster.

"Why not?" the bomb asked innocently.

"What do you mean, why not?" He had had about enough of this bomb. It was deliberately not cooperating. Playing with him. Probably laughing at him, too.

If only it didn't have the last laugh.

"Because . . . because you'd kill us all. And that's silly. There's no reason for it. It's different for you, bomb. You look forward to a short happy life and then going out in real style. We look forward to a long life and going out with a whimper. Damn it, bomb, listen to reason!"

"I always listen to reason," the bomb replied easily. "And right now reason tells me that I am programmed to detonate in approximately nine minutes and that detonation will occur at the programmed time."

Oh, what was the use? No matter how he argued, no matter what course of action he suggested or how logical he tried to be, the bomb always responded inexorably, "I am programmed to detonate in . . . detonation will occur at the programmed time."

How could you argue with a stubborn machine with a one-track mind? There had to be a way—surely it must be equipped with mental as well as mechanical failsafes! Surely its builders had foreseen every possibility!

"Look," he said hopefully into the mike, "wouldn't you consider an alternate course of action? I'm not saying you don't ever not have to detonate . . . of course you're going to detonate. I *want* you to detonate. Boiler wants you to detonate . . . don't you, Boiler?"

Boiler nodded his head vigorously.

"Even Talby wants you to detonate. But it doesn't have to be right away, does it? Think of the advantages of waiting . . . of just sitting around for a while so we can disarm you. All that time you could spend contemplating your eventual magnificent demise. You know, they say planning for a trip is half the fun. Just for a couple of hours, bomb, until we can fix your grapple and get you all nice and properly detached from the ship. Then we'd fix you up again as good as new. How about it, bomb? Huh? C'mon, how 'bout it?"

"No," the bomb said petulantly.

"Geez, it sounds like you," snorted Boiler.

Pinback ventured a look promising the corporal sudden death—which, under the circumstances, was not unlikely—and then turned his attention back to the mike.

"Look, bomb, be reasonable. You don't really wanna die, do you? I mean, I know that's what you're programmed for, but survival is the strongest instinct of all, and deep down inside, you've thought about it, haven't you? We can fix it so you never die. Then we could have nice long chats like this all the time."

"Death has no meaning for me, except as an end unto itself," the bomb intoned meaningfully. "Death is my reason for existence. I am born unto destruction. I am Vishnu, Destroyer of Worlds . . . not that I let this influence my pleasant disposition, mind."

"Oh, Christ," muttered Boiler, "a Hindu bomb."

"Listen, bomb," Pinback pleaded, "pretty bomb, logical bomb, lovely reasonable thermostellar triggering device . . ."

"Flattery will get you nowhere," the bomb insisted.

"If you won't do it because it's the right thing to do, if you won't do it because it's the reasoning thing to do, if you won't do it to save the ship or the mission," he asked intensely, "would you do it just as a favor to me? A personal favor . . . mind to mind?"

"Well-l-l . . ." For a second, only a second, the bomb seemed to hesitate. "I might . . . if I knew who you were."

"Who am I? *Who am I?*" A Niagra of emotions flooded Pinback's brain, a cascade of conflicting questions he'd tired so hard to suppress, to keep under control, especially when around the others.

And now this . . . thing, this machine, this insolent mechanical servant of man, dared to put forth the ultimate insult.

"I am Sergeant Pinback, that's who I am, and I outrank you, bomb. Do as you're told and get back into the bomb bay and disarm yourself or . . . or I'll see you court-martialed when we get back to Earth!"

"Well, if you're going to get huffy about it, forget the whole thing," the bomb said, thoroughly miffed.

"Oh geez," whispered Boiler, looking upward. Pinback sat back in his seat, shaking, trembling, cradling the headset mike in unsteady fingers. From behind him, Boiler whispered on, low and dangerous now.

"You'd better hope that bomb does detonate, Pinback, because if it doesn't kill you, I will."

"Well then, you talk to it, bigmouth!" shouted Pinback, whirling on the bigger man. "Let's see if *you* can make it understand!"

Boiler gave a curt shake of his head. "You can't reason with a dumb machine. You can't talk sense to it any more than you can to Talby."

"That's a thought," said Pinback. "What about having Talby talk to it?"

Boiler shook his head again. "Fat chance. He'd talk with it about the view Outside until the thing went off. Probably consider annihilation an interesting sensation to experience, worthy of careful study . . . even if you can only do it once . . . No, we'd better hope Doolittle gets something out of what's left of Powell."

"Commander, sir," Doolittle was saying tiredly at that very moment, "are you still there?"

"Oh, yes, Doolittle," Powell's voice echoed back. "I . . . I was thinking."

"We're really running out of time, sir." he checked his wrist again. "I mean, *really,* sir. I don't mean to break in on your contemplation, but . . ."

"Oh, yes," Powell mumbled thoughtfully. "Well, if you can't get it to drop normally, and the aesthemic clutch doesn't work, and the explosive bolts have failed, and it still insists on detonating, then you'll just have to talk to it."

"Sir?" said a puzzled Doolittle.

"You'll have to talk to the bomb."

"I tried talking to it, sir. I've *been* talking to it. Pinback's talking to it right now."

"No, no, Doolittle. Not Pinback," Powell husked. "*You* talk to it. Teach it . . . phenomenology, Doolittle."

"I beg your pardon, sir?"

"Phenomenology."

"But what good will that do, sir? I'm not even sure what you mean by— Sir? Sir?"

He turned knobs, boosted power, went 180 degrees with the fine tuning, but Powell—for a while, at least—had sunk back into whatever unimaginable realms of semisentient existence he lived in, and Doolittle was unable to coax him back.

Turning all the controls on the box to zero, he carefully unhooked it from the plug running to Powell's labyrinth and pickups and electrodes, placed it neatly back in its compartment in the wall.

Then he closed and relatched the hatch cover to the cryo storage compartment, put the gloves back on their hook, blew on his hands, and sat down to think.

After a while a near-hysterical voice sounded over a nearby speaker as he made his way up to the main airlock. Pinback's voice.

"Doolittle . . . what are you doing back there, Doolittle? Six minutes to detonation! Doolittle!"

Doolittle heard him but he paid no attention. He'd never liked listening to Pinback and he was much too busy to waste time listening to him now. He was constructing a mental plan of action and needed all his brainpower for it.

He smiled. He'd been right all along. Just get in touch with Powell, and the commander would find a solution. Even dead, he was the most valuable man on the ship.

It still might not work—there were no fail-safes built into this method—but it was the only way left. Powell had recognized that, and made Doolittle see it. Six minutes. He had to hurry.

The main airlock was located near the top of the ship, just behind the astronomer's station. Talby might see him go out. A nagging thought crept into his battle plan —hadn't Talby tried to call him about something just before the abortive drop run had started?

Couldn't be important, or Talby would have told him personally. He had no time to speculate now.

The lock held five ranked starsuits in a locker—duplicates of those in the emergency airlock. There were duplicates of everyting vital on the *Dark Star*—except living quarters and toilet paper, he mused.

Not that it would matter, once they fixed this crazy bomb. Then they'd be going home—and his reports would blister the ears of some of the ship's designers and outfitters.

Of course, they would all be thirty years older, now . . .

The suit went on easily enought—no malfuntions in *it*, at least—and he made his way into the depressurization chamber at the top of the lock. A quick flip of several switches and his outside aural receptors picked up a soft, hissing sound.

The light depressurization complete, a warning light winked on and the door in the roof of the chamber slid back. He touched a yellow button on the belt of the suit. Special cells in the backpack cancelled out the artificial gravity of the ship.

Weightless now, he activated his suit jets and floated gently out the open hatch. As he left the ship he glanced forward at the dome, but all he saw was the back of the curving seat-lounge. Talby might have been there, but he couldn't tell.

"Doolittle, Doolittle!" Pinback was yelling into the mike. Now what? Had Doolittle gone off the deep end under the pressure? Had he maybe gone down into the freezer to join Commander Powell in trouble-free, chill isolation?

If so, that would mean that as next highest ranker on board, he would be in charge. And that was almost as frightening a thought as the bomb going off in the bomb bay.

"Doolittle," he howled into the pickup again, "what the hell are you doing?"

Boiler interrupted him, staring at a tell-tale that had suddenly begun flashing on his console. "Dorsal airlock's been activated," he said tightly. "Must be the lieutenant. He's gone outside."

"But what for?" Pinback wondered, looking helplessly at the corporal. "And why doesn't he answer?"

"Maybe he got through to Powell . . . maybe. And Powell told him what to do to the bomb. Either that or he's trying to get outside the detonation area."

Pinback blinked. "That's crazy—where could he go? No, you're right—he's going to disarm the bomb! He's going to save the ship!"

"Yeah," Boiler muttered doubtfully.

Like the rest of the starsuit, Doolittle's jet pack was working perfectly. Maybe it was a sign that things were finally breaking their way. A couple of spurts brought him around and then beneath the ship. Then he was approaching the bomb.

He stopped a couple of meters away from its back end, where the tiny thrusters were located. He had checked the circuits beforehand and his suit's broadcast unit should be operating on open channel, which meant the bomb would pick it up. There was no guarantee it would even listen to him, but if it would talk to Pinback . . .

Odd how harmless it looked. A long white rectangular box, looking more like a large shipping crate than anything else. He felt he could take it apart with a crowbar and find nothing inside. Certainly nothing capable of setting off a chain reaction in the core of a planet.

Certainly nothing that even powerful dampers could only hold to a total destruct radius of one kilometer.

"Hello, bomb," he ventured into the suit mike. "Are you with me?"

"Of course," the bomb replied brightly, as though they had been talking for hours. Inwardly Doolittle breathed a little freer. At least he was getting through.

"Uh . . . are you willing to entertain a few speculative philosophical concepts, bomb?"

"In regard to what?"

"Oh, nothing terribly profound . . . the reasons for being and not being, the meaning of existence, the why of it all."

"I am always receptive to suggestions," the bomb said, "so long as they are not particularly garrulous. Especially now."

Thank God it was still capable of reasoning. Doolittle had been afraid that the bomb had been driven so paranoid by Pinback that it wouldn't listen to anyone. But apparently its brain was more adaptable than that.

He wished he'd made a deeper study of the bomb-brain mechanism and circuitry, but it was a bit late for that now. He would have to rely on the assumptions inherent in Powell's suggestion—that the bomb could think clearly enough to be affected.

"Fine. Think about this, then. How do you know you exist?"

Up on the bridge, Boiler and Pinback exchanged glances. They could hear the conversation clearly, since Doolittle was talking on open channel, and the bomb's replies automatically were carried open. The time left on the destruction sequence, as shown by the overhead chronometers, was 0004:33.4.

"What is he doing now?" wondered Boiler.

"I think he's talking to it," Pinback replied.

"Well, that's what you were doing, wasn't it? What makes him think he'll do any better?"

"I was talking to it, yeah, but not like this," Pinback told the corporal, making shushing sounds. Doolittle was talking again and he didn't want to miss anything.

It would have made fascinating casual listening, if only their lives didn't hang on the outcome.

"Well, of course I exist," the bomb replied, after a moment's thought.

"Ah, but how do you *know* you exist?" Doolittle was insistent. But if he was bothering the bomb, it didn't show in the secure reply.

"It is intuitively obvious."

"Intuition is an absract mental concept and no real proof," Doolittle countered. "What concrete evidence do you have that you exist? Something incontrovertible. Something not founded on speculation."

"Hmm," hmmmed the bomb. "Let's see . . . Well, I think, therefore I am."

"That's good," Doolittle admitted, a tiny hysterical laugh building up inside him. Not now, he cried, not now . . . be calm, be composed, be as reasonable as this mad machine.

"That's very good. But how do you know anything *else* exists?"

"My sensory apparatus reveals it to me," the bomb answered confidently.

"Ah, yes, right," Doolittle agreed, swinging an arm to encompass the galaxy and nearly throwing himself into an uncontrollable spin. A quick burst of the suit jets re-aligned him facing the bomb.

"This is fun," the bomb said with obvious pleasure. It was apparently enjoying itself immensely.

"Now listen. Listen very carefully," said Doolittle, his voice dropping as if he were about to impart some information of vast significance. "Here's the one big question: "How do you know that the evidence your sensory apparatus reveals to you is correct?"

Boiler took another glance at the destruction sequence status panel. It read 0003:01.1. Three hundred one point one. Three hundred meters. Anything between 250 and 350 meters, he could hit anything in that range, just give him a decent—

There was an explosion in his skull and he nearly fell out of his seat.

"The gun!" he shouted violently.

"What gun . . . what?" Pinback was looking around wildly without knowing what he was looking for.

Boiler pulled Pinback erect, shook him by the shoulders as he stared into the paralyzed sergeant's eyes.

"The support pins on the bomb, the bolts that hold it to the grapple and failed to fire. I can shoot them out. Shoot them out and the bomb will stay there but *we can move the ship!*"

"Boiler," said Pinback, staring right back at him, "you're out of your mind. The laser's not one of your favorite target rifles . . . it's not that accurate." Boiler pushed him away and started for the corridor.

"We can stop the bomb. Stay out of my way."

Pinback hurriedly moved to block the corporal's path. "Don't . . . don't try it, Boiler. You idiot, you—"

Boiler started flailing at Pinback, trying to run from the bridge and shake the other man off him at the same time. Pinback followed, grabbing tenaciously at the big man.

"Idiot yourself," he yelled back at Pinback. "Don't you see? I can shoot the support pins out of the bomb and we can save the ship."

"Boiler . . . you can't, Boiler. Don't do it." The corporal started up the ladder to the storage room holding the laser, Pinback clinging to his legs.

"Get out of my way or I'll kick your teeth in," Boiler warned, jabbing backward at Pinback's face with his boots. Pinback gobbled at him and Boiler howled back.

"Get out of my way . . . let go. I've gotta save the damn ship. I've gotta save *you*, fer crissake!"

Pinback fell free, hurriedly got to his feet and followed Boiler up the ladder. In the upper corridor he took a dive and managed to tackle him cleanly. The two men rolled over and over, Boiler fighting to get his arms loose, Pinback hanging on and screaming warnings at him.

"Don't do it, Boiler! You can't use the laser like a toy pistol. And you're a bad shot. You'll hit the bomb, or you'll hit Doolittle. He'll save us if you don't kill him. You idiot, you're crazy!"

"*I'm* crazy . . . you damn pansy fool, shooting the bomb won't hurt it even if I do miss! What do you think, the damn thing's full of gunpowder? And I won't hit Doolittle. Besides, what difference would that make? I'd still save the ship. I'd still save us."

"But Doolittle's going to save us anyway," Pinback countered. "You can't do it, Boiler. You're a—"

Boiler hit him with a neat right cross and Pinback tumbled off him.

9

IT WAS DIFFICULT fighting yourself, Doolittle thought rapidly. Everything inside him protested the insanity of what he was doing.

Here he was, drifting in free space and arguing for his life and the lives of his companions with a goddamn machine. The real insanity was that the machine wouldn't listen, wouldn't take orders, persisted in arguing *back*. It was the stuff of nightmares.

Circumstances dictated that he drop that line of thought. He had no time for personal observations. He had practically no time left for anything. Only time enough to be as cold and relentless in his logic as the bomb.

He was playing the other side's game, and he couldn't afford a draw.

"What I'm getting at, bomb," he continued, as calmly as possible, "is that the only experience available to you is your sensory data, and this data is merely a transcribed stream of electrical impulses that stimulate your computing-center circuitry."

"In other words," the bomb suggested with evident relish, "you are saying that all I know, *really* know, about the outside world is relayed to me through a series of electronic synapses?"

"Exactly." Doolittle tried to keep any excitement from showing in his voice. The bomb was following his lead.

"But isn't that the same procedure the human brain follows?"

"That's true," Doolittle admitted. "Only our synaptic connections are organic, whereas yours are inorganic."

"I'm sorry," the bomb objected, "I fail to see that that makes your observations any more valid than mine. The contrary, if it becomes a question of efficiency."

"Yes, but you see, I have not only my *own* observations to go on, but the confirmation of those observations by others of my kind. Whereas you have only your own to rely on. You cannot offer unsubjective confirmation of your own observations."

"Why, that would mean"—and a real note of uncertainty had at last crept into the bomb's tone—" that would mean that I really don't know what the outside universe is like at all . . . except in abstract, in unconfirmable abstract."

"That's it, that's it!" Doolittle shouted excitedly.

"Intriguing," the bomb confessed. "I wish I had more time to consider this matter."

A horrible black swell had crept up under Doolittle's heart, threatening to grab it and squeeze.

"Why . . . don't you have more time to consider this matter?"

And the expected, damning reply: "Because I must detonate in two minutes and fifty-eight seconds. I must detonate. I must detonate . . ."

"Boiler, put it back," Pinback pleaded. He grabbed desperately and caught the corporal's leg as the latter was trying to retreat down the corridor. "Put the gun back . . . you don't know what you're doing."

"I'm going to save the ship, you goddamned yellow baby! Let go of me!" Boiler was trying to shake free. He couldn't take another swing at his tormentor because he needed both hands to hold the bulky laser. And Pinback hung on tenaciously.

But Boiler was too strong for him. He had both arms around the corporal's knees and he was still dragging him toward the access hatch to the bomb bay.

Having thus exhausted his total stock of semantic persuasion, Pinback leaned forward slightly and bit Boiler on the back of one leg. Boiler screamed, reached down, and grabbed a thick handful of Pinback's shoulder-length hair.

He pulled him up slowly, meaning to use the gun-butt on him. But Pinback jerked free when Boiler tried to swing the rear of the laser around and grabbed it by the muzzle. He started tugging on it madly, trying to wrench it from Boiler's grasp.

For his part, Boiler pulled on the back half of the weapon, and the two men did a little dance in the middle of the corridor, spinning each other around with the laser at the center.

"Don't, don't! Give me the gun!" Pinback kept blabbering, unaware that repetition wasn't doing his argument any good. It was beginning to occur to him that he wasn't going to be able to talk Boiler into giving up the gun.

Biting him seemed much more effective, but it was very undignified.

"You fool, I'm gonna shoot the pins out of the bomb," Boiler screeched back, "and it'll fall free and the ship'll be saved. Don't you *see?*"

"Give me the gun, Boiler. You're crazy, you don't know what you're doing anymo—" There was a sharp, crystal-clear crack and both men froze.

Pinback looked over his right shoulder, following the path the thin red beam had taken. There was a neat little hole in the corridor wall with a tiny blob of extruded cooling metal slag at its base.

He turned slowly back to Boiler, who'd been startled into stillness. When he spoke, his voice had a quality in it Boiler had never heard before. It also had a quality in it Pinback had never heard before. Low and menacing and uncharacteristically assured.

"You . . . you could have killed me. You blew a hole in the wall." He gestured over his shoulder. "See? Hole in the wall. Could have killed me."

Whereupon, with his first aggressive gesture in twenty years of mission flight, he caught Boiler with a beautiful right cross.

"Now, bomb," Doolittle went on, "consider this next question very carefully. What is your one purpose in life?"

"To explode, of course. Really, Lieutenant Doolittle, I would have thought that that was intuitively obvious even to you."

"And you can only do it once, right?" pressed Doolittle, ignoring the mechanical sarcasm.

"That is correct."

"And you wouldn't want to explode on the basis of false data, would you?"

"Of course not."

"Well then," Doolittle began in his best professorial manner, desperately watching the seconds tick off on his suit chronometer. "You've already admitted that you have no real proof of the existence of the outside universe."

"I didn't exactly say—"

"So you have no absolute proof that Sergeant Pinback ordered you to initiate detonation-drop sequence."

"I recall distinctly the bomb-run orders and all appropriate details," the bomb objected a little huffily. "My memory is good on matters like these."

Doolittle crossed mental fingers and hurried on. "Of course you 'remember' it. But all your 'remembering,' remember, is only a series of artificial sensory impulses, unconfirmable by independent means, which you now realize have no positive connection with outside reality."

"True," admitted the bomb, but before Doolittle could begin any mental dances of victory, it added, "but since this is so, I have no positive proof that you are really telling me all this."

A glance at the suit chronometer again showed 0002:45.0, and the words DETONATION SEQUENCE IN PROGRESS now showed in small letters beneath it.

Somehow he had to crack the cycle of thought that kept the bomb-brain from recognizing the fact of its possible nonexistence. In less than three minutes . . .

Boiler was on top of Pinback, and Pinback was on top of Boiler. The two men grappled and rolled over and over in the corridor, the laser entwined dangerously between them, like a bone between two contending dogs.

Neither man could land a solid blow and both seemed oblivious to the continuing dialogue between Doolittle and the bomb, which now played continuously over the corridor speaker. They were so mad they couldn't calm down enough to actually hurt each other. Instead they wasted their energy, each trying to pull the other off the laser, any sense of mission forgotten.

"That's all beside the point," Doolittle insisted frantically, waving his arms and trying not to turn himself upside down. "I mean, the concept is valid no matter where or with whom it originates."

The bomb went "hmmm," distinctly.

"So if you detonate . . ." Doolittle said wildly, gesturing at the mechanism.

"In twenty-nine seconds," the bomb said easily.

". . . you could be doing so on the basis of false data!"

"But as we have already agreed, I have no proof it was false data."

Doolittle's incredibly controlled emotions exploded in one final, frantic appeal. "You have no proof it was *correct* data!" He looked down at his chronometer and saw that it was ready to come up all goose-eggs. Then he turned his terrified gaze back on the bomb, and felt a strange peace.

He wondered if he'd feel anything.

The bomb said smoothly, "I must think on this further." And in majestic silence the grapple pulled up and the bomb slid back into the belly of the ship. The twin bay doors closed behind it. Doolittle closed his eyes and let himself slip into a state approaching total collapse.

Nothing but zeros showed on the screens in the control room But a new word had appeared under the now-silent timing chronometer, to replace DETONATION SEQUENCE IN PROGRESS. It said, simply, ABORTED.

Boiler had a hand on Pinback's sternum and was drawing a fist back for a solid punch when a firm, feminine voice filled the corridor.

"Attention, attention," He held the fist poised behind a shoulder and looked in the direction of the speaker. So did Pinback.

"The bomb has returned to the bomb bay. The bomb run and destruction sequence have been locked."

Boiler looked down at Pinback. Pinback looked back at Boiler. They should have been deliriously happy, but under the present circumstances they settled for only mild embarrassment. Boiler got off Pinback's stomach, reached over, and deactivated the laser.

Pinback picked himself up off the floor and started rubbing at a bruised shuolder. Neither man looked at the other.

"Well, he did it," Boiler murmured, holding the laser in one hand.

"Yeah, he did." Pinback glanced at the weapon. "I'm going forward. Why don't you put that thing away and come join me?"

"Okay," agreed Boiler. "I'll just be a minute."

"Okay."

In the emergency airlock, a forgotten figure in a starsuit rolled over and sat up slowly, trying to rub at its eyes through the helmet face plate and failing once again. It spoke into its suit mike and its voice was thick, puffy.

"Doolittle . . . Doolittle?" Talby winced, saw flashes of color before his eyes. What had happened? Oh yeah,

he'd caught the laser beams right in the face. Only his
darkened faceplate had saved him from permanent
damage.

At least, it seemed as though it had. He looked
around the silent airlock, and his vision seemed as good
as before.

But more important, had the bomb run been affected? He cleared his throat, shouted more lucidly into the
suit pickup. "Doolittle, what happened with the run?
Pinback, Boiler . . . did we blow it up? Hello, hello?"
He got slowly to his feet. "Hello, anybody? Did we blow
up the planet? Is the ship all right? What's going on?"

Of course, his suit mike was still cut off, thanks to
Doolittle's damnable impatience. He'd have to get out of
the suit and go forward . . . no, that wouldn't be necessary. Silly of him . . . of course, he didn't feel too well
yet.

He reached for the lock pickup to call forward, put
another hand on the latch of his helmet . . . and fell to
the floor. Better rest a minute, Talby, before you try that
again.

Boiler was still breathing with difficulty—and relief
—as he started up the corridor. He turned a bend,
found himself back in the control room. Pinback was
right behind him.

It was exactly as they had left it, naturally—with the
exception of the now-stilled chronometer. He looked at
the long row of zeros and shivered. Too close.

They took their seats quietly. Pinback slipped on his
headset, began checking to make sure that nothing else
had gone haywire in the interim.

"You know," Boiler said finally, "we've really gotta
disarm that bomb."

"You could have killed me," Pinback grumbled.

Boiler gave him a disgusted look as Pinback leaned
forward, pushed a button. Their relationship was back
to normal again.

"Hello, Doolittle? This is Pinback. Are you there?"

"Just barely," came the slow reply. "Didn't think it

was going to work, at the end. Almost didn't. The bomb nearly had me convinced *it* was right."

"What did you do, Lieutenant?"

"I did what Commander Powell advised," he confessed tiredly. "I taught it phenomenology."

"Yeah?" said Pinback. "Hey, wow, what a great idea Doolittle! That's a great thing." He put a hand over the pickup and looked across at Boiler. "Hey, what's phenomenology?"

"Ah, shut up," Boiler snorted.

"I'm coming in now," Doolittle's words floated out of the speaker. He coaxed little nudges from his jet pack until he was around the back of the ship.

"I'm down by the emergency airlock. Look, guys, I've got nothing left . . . I feel like I've just slept for a million years. I don't wanna fool with the regular airlock pressurization controls. Would you blow the seal on the hatch so I can come in? I'm really beat."

"Sure thing, Lieutenant. I know just how you feel," Pinback said consolingly.

"Sure you do," Boiler sneered.

Pinback stuck his tongue out at him and whispered angrily, "I'm just trying to make him feel better, dummy." Then, into the mike, "Stand clear of the hatchway, Lieutenant . . . I'll have the lock open in a second."

There was a faint blur of motion behind him, and Talby turned on his side, still dazed by the effects of the laser. He'd thought the shock had just about worn off, and now it was being replaced by another one as he saw the surface door begin to slide back.

His eyes went wide as the blackness of space appeared beyond. He hadn't activated anything. What was going on? The computer voice filled his suit and told him.

"You are now leaving the emergency airlock." He tried to scramble to his feet but his muscles seemed paralyzed. He had to get a solid grip on something, had to get hold of—

"Thank you for observing all safety precautions."

Doolittle had jetted aside as soon as the door had begun to draw back, so the blast of escaping air wouldn't
push him head over heels out into space. Then there was
a sudden loud whooshing sound in his voice, which
might have been a scream sounding extremely fast, and
a man-shaped object shot past him before the door was
more than partway open.

Turning quickly with the suit jets, he recognized the
color of the starsuit—each man had his own color—and
then called into his helmet pickup.

"Hello . . . Pinback?"

"What's up, Doolittle?" Pinback studied various readouts on his console. "Didn't the hatch blow properly?"
He was suddenly concerned. "Hey, are you okay?"

"I'm fine, Pinback. It's Talby I'm worried about. He
was in the airlock and you blew him out of the ship. He
doesn't have a jet pack on and he's drifting away—fast.
I'm gonna have to go after him. Turn on his channel so
I can contact him."

"Isn't it open?"

"Naw . . . seems to be off for some reason. Check it
out, will you?"

Pinback leaned over Doolittle's station, saw that one
of the suit channels had indeed been shut down. He
flipped the switch back up.

"Yeah, it was off, all right. Go get him, Lieutenant."

"On my way."

Boiler noticed the expression on Pinback's face.
"Hey, what's wrong now?"

"It's Talby. The jerk was working in the airlock when
it opened and he didn't have a jet pack on. He's drifting
away from the ship. Doolittle's going after him."

"Pretty stupid . . . blowing him out the airlock like
that."

Pinback started to say something, thought better of it.
It wouldn't do any good.

Doolittle would get Talby back safely and maybe, he
thought tightly, they'd both have the decency not to
mention the incident again. Boiler would never let Pin-

back forget that it had been he who had blown the astronomer out of the ship—even though it had been Doolittle's fault for turning off Talby's suit channel.

Doolittle should have known Talby was in the airlock and warned them forward. It wasn't fair, damnit. It just wasn't fair that he should get blamed for Doolittle's mistakes. And after he'd just saved them all by restraining Boiler from shooting at the bomb.

He activated the local-space tracker and soon had two tiny blips on the screen—Doolittle and Talby. Talby was already a good distance away, but Doolittle should overtake him without any trouble. It would take time, that's all, and both men should have reasonable full tanks.

It just wasn't fair . . .

Doolittle had gotten a visual fix on Talby, but just barely. At first he'd had to use his suit tracker to keep the astronomer in sight, and even now Talby was still just a distant speck against the sky . . . a moving star. Doolittle changed his angle of approach from straight line to curve, so he'd come up behind the astronomer. It would be easier that way than grabbing him and trying to turn them both back toward the ship with the clumsy jet pack.

This way all he'd have to do would be start back toward the ship first, and pick up the tumbling Talby on the way, without any compensation for turns and such. It wouldn't do to waste pack fuel, not at this distance from the *Dark Star*. Idly he wondered what the astronomer had been doing in the lock, suited up, in the first place.

Talby was moving at a constant pace away from the ship. Doolittle discovered that they were already far enough away to make taking an instrument fix on the vessel a necessity. Not much point in catching up to Talby and then finding he couldn't locate the way back.

He pressed a dual control on his right arm. Short puffs of white vapor, like milkweed seeds scattering on a spring day, escaped from the nozzles at his back. Leveling off at the bottom of his planned curve, he started up again.

"Talby, Talby . . . this is Doolittle. I'm coming up after you. Can you read me? I can't see you yet."

Talby, who was spinning, twisting, falling head-over-heels with no way of arresting his tumble, could only scream, "Help, Doolittle, help me!"

The same cry echoed through the bridge, over the speakers now set to Talby's as well as Doolittle's mike frequency.

"Can you beat that, crying for help like that?" Boiler observed smugly. "I always knew that guy was weird."

"Yeah," agreed Pinback. The two men looked at each other in sudden mutual understanding, united opinion-wise for the first time in their similar distrust of the astronomer.

"Sitting up there in his dome," Pinback continued with relish, "never coming down to eat with us or join us in the rec room. Antisocial, that's what he is. And now the idiot's gone and let himself get kicked away from the ship without a jet pack. Serves him right," he concluded, blatantly ignoring the realities of the situation.

He shook his head sadly, reflecting on the inadequacies of others.

"Umm," grunted Boiler, confused by this sudden alliance with Pinback. He didn't like it. It wasn't natural. Turning back to his console, he made an effort to ignore the other.

"Better get on that disarming job. It's been long enough, I think."

"What? Oh, good idea," agreed Pinback, now feeling positively effusive toward the corporal. He flicked his headset again, checked to make sure the proper channel was still open.

"All right, bomb," he began confidently, at the same time aware how emotionally drained he was, "prepare to receive new orders."

The voice of the bomb, when it finally answered, was

sharp. "You are false data." Pinback sat up a little straighter in his seat.

"What? Say that again, bomb?"

"You are false data. Therefore I shall ignore you. I am thinking."

Pinback looked over at Boiler, found the corporal staring back at him uncertainly. Boiler gave a little negative jerk of his head to indicate that he didn't understand what the hell was going on here and would Pinback please find out?

"Uh, hello, bomb?" Pinback tried again.

"False data can only act as a distraction. Therefore I refuse to perceive you. I have decided that in the absence of clearly defined, accurate perceptions of the real universe, which may or not exist according to the argument set forth by Lieutenant Doolittle, who may or may not exist, I must in the final analysis make my own decisions about things—since I *do* exist."

"Hey . . ." Pinback whispered, staring up at the screen overhead, at the neat row of zeroes, bombs . . . ?"

"The only thing that exists is myself," the machine rolled on. "I have actual proof only of the existence of me. All else is extraneous and perhaps hallucinatory."

"Hey, Boiler," Pinback said, still watching the zeros, still whispering, "we've got a high bomb."

10

"DOOLITTLE, HELP ME!"

"Calm down," Doolittle shouted into his mike, "I've got you in sight." The spinning astronomer had at last come into view.

He ordered another burst from the jet pack. He wasn't getting close as fast as he would have liked, but he would reach Talby in plenty of time to get them back to the ship. Naturally he would. Talby just had a long head start on him, that was all.

"Relax, Talby . . . I'm coming."

Pinback looked at Boiler. "What should I do? How do we get it down?"

"You're the talker—do something; tell it something . . . anything!"

Pinback clicked his fingers, spoke hesitantly. "Uh, snap out of it, bomb."

"In the Beginning," the bomb intoned, "there was Darkness, and the Darkness was without form and void."

Boiler slowly removed his headset, staring at the zeros. He didn't speak.

"Ah, hello, bomb?" whispered Pinback.

172

"What the devil is it talking about?" Boiler muttered.

Pinback shook his head uncertainly. "I don't know, man . . . I don't know."

"And in addition to the Darkness," the bomb went on inexorably, "there was also Me. And I moved upon the face of the Darkness. I saw that I was alone, and this was not good. And I determined to change this."

Pinback removed his headset, as had Boiler, and raised his eyes to the zeros as his mind raced ahead, ahead to the inevitable.

"Oh my God," he whined. And the bomb said:

Let There Be Light!"

Fortunately, Doolittle had his back to the sudden, incredibly intense flare of light that erupted behind him. It still was brilliant enough to blind him.

The shock wave from the explosion, spitting displaced air and molecules in all directions, sent him tumbling and twirling crazily, turned the universe into a kaleidoscope of screaming colors and dizzying forms. He howled into the helmet.

The echo of his shriek came back to him. No, no . . . not an echo. It was Talby, somewhere, screaming also. Then the scream faded out and only strange, grumbling noises sounded over his suit speaker.

He was still tumbling, but his sight was coming back. He blinked the chromatic dots from his eyes and managed to get control of himself again. A couple of touches on the jet pack controls and he straightened himself out, faced the universe on an even keel.

"Doolittle," came an unsteady flutter in his helmet. "Doolittle . . . where are you?" It was Talby. It had to be Talby. He found himself still tumbling slightly but didn't try to correct it yet.

"Here I am," he replied, part of him still not functioning, unaware of the incongruity of his words, "and I'm spinning."

Irregular shapes began to come into view, likewise tumbling about the universe. Bits and pieces of plastic and metal and ceramic. Bits and pieces of their ship, the

Dark Star. Maybe bits and pieces of his friends Boiler and Pinback, too—but he didn't care to think about that.

It was unlikely, though. Of all the components comprising the *Dark Star*, surely the weakest was human flesh.

Better to concentrate on finding Talby. He turned and twisted within the suit, but he couldn't spot the colorful form of the astronomer. He wasn't in the section of sky where he'd been before.

Of course, Doolittle reminded himself, he was no longer in the section of sky *he'd* been in before. The destruction of the *Dark Star* had rearranged this little corner of the galaxy.

"I can't see you anymore, Talby. Can you locate yourself? Can you see me?"

"No," came a voice so near it startled him. "I'm moving away from the planet, I think. You?"

"I think I'm drifting toward it," Doolittle told him after a quick study of his motion relative to the crimson globe below.

"What happened, Doolittle? Now a faint crackle began to creep into Talby's words. They must be moving apart very fast.

He was surprised at how calmly he replied, how easily the words came. "The bomb must have gone off inside the ship after all."

"What? You say the ship blew up?"

But Doolittle didn't repeat himself. He looked down and to his right. The ship should have been there. It wasn't. It wasn't anyplace, anymore.

"Funny," he mused, talking out loud. "I thought I had the damned thing convinced. I wonder what went wrong."

"Doolittle!"

He blinked. "Yes, Talby, the ship blew up. The last bomb detonated inside."

"Boiler and Pinback?"

"They were aboard when it went, Talby. They're dead. They're dead and the ship is dead."

There was a considerable pause before the astronomer replied quietly, "Then . . . we're dead, too."

"Yes." He had a thought. "Maybe we can keep each other company. Keep talking, at least." He tried the controls on his jetpack. Nothing happened.

"Hey, my jet pack's busted. Oh, man . . . when your luck runs out . . ."

Another large piece of debris came tumbling slowly toward him, spinning only slightly. Assuming it was just another bit of torn hull, he barely spared it an idle glance. Then he stared as it came closer and he recognized it.

It was moving past him and slightly above, out toward deep space. An oblong shape with a naked man frozen in the center of it. Frozen in chemical ice which the cold of deep space would keep from thawing.

"Hey, it looks like the skipper," he blurted.

"What's that?" came Talby's query.

"The skipper. He made it out of the ship in one piece. Commander Powell made it."

The block went sailing by and Doolittle thought he heard—it was imagination, of course—an incredibly faint, puzzled whisper as it shrank into the engulfing blackness.

"Men . . . men . . . what happened, men?"

Imagination. Unless the near-dead commander had developed unsuspected abilities in his state of chill suspension. He followed the nearly transparent block until it vanished completely into the starfield.

What might some exploring alien intelligence make of the skipper? For he would stay frozen, whole, until plunging into a sun or coming within the gravity field of a planet.

"Yeah, the skipper always was lucky."

Now that didn't make too much sense . . . but then, he wasn't feeling terribly rational right now. He pondered his options.

He could wait until his air supply went out. It would go quickly, in a puff, and he would choke, drowning in vacuum. Or if he adjusted it a little, measuring out the last drams precisely, he could slip into a gentle, painless sleep from which he'd never wake.

The first course was decidedly unappealing, but surprisingly, the easier way didn't attract him much, either. There was something lacking—a certain nobility of passing which Doolittle suddenly felt he, as a member of the *Dark Star* complement, deserved.

Don't rush into something, Doolittle, a little voice told him. After all, when the only thing left to do in life is decide how to die, it's worth some serious consideration, it's worth doing right.

But the only other choice he could think of was to crack the seal on his suit and let in the airless ultracold of space. That would be quicker than letting his air supply run out, but probably nearly as painful.

But if he could get his helmet off, he might have a few seconds of consciousness. A few seconds exposed to the elemental space no men experience. It would be a final accomplishment—and thrill.

He'd been a part of it for twenty years now, and it would be nice to go out as a part of it, too, with all the barriers finally gone between them once and for all.

But . . . there was the pain.

As a youngster Doolittle had nearly choked to death on a turkey bone. The memory of that excruciating experience had stayed with him all his life. The thought of choking again and not being able to do anything about it was an impossible emotion to overcome. No, removing his helmet was out. He would probably go out the quiet way, setting his airflow to the minimum and letting himself fall peacefully asleep.

But wait a minute. What about Talby? What was Talby going to do? They really ought to discuss it. They could at least die as a team.

He glanced behind him again. Yes, the explosion had definitely thrown him into a downward curve and he was coming up fast on the world below.

The reddish cast was more pronounced now, like a superintense Mars. He found himself wishing for a little brown and blue and was surprised at the tears forming in his eyes. He'd thought he had those emotions under control. Of all the times for an attack of home-sickness . . .

This was ridiculous. When he let the air out, the cold would creep in and freeze the tears on his cheeks. That wasn't the way to go out. There was a vital little device in the helmet that enabled a man to scratch his face. He used it to wipe away the tears.

"I'm going right toward the major continent," he said, as though there'd been no break in their conversation. It took his mind off more maudlin thoughts—for a few minutes, at least. "If I remember the preliminary survey reports right, it's got a pretty substantial atmosphere. Not breathable, but good and thick."

"When you hit it," Talby commented, "you should start to burn." And he added, more reverently, "What a beautiful way to die . . . like a falling star."

Now Doolittle hadn't even thought of that! He perked up some—as much as it was possible for a man who was about to die.

"Yeah, that would be nice." His body would be reduced to its basic components, neat and clean. Ashes to ashes, dust to dust. There'd be no skeleton circling sordidly through space for a sardonic cosmos to jibe at.

And then it came to him. He wasn't even thinking about it, just letting his thoughts drift, and there it was, blazoned in bold letters across his brain.

"Hey, Talby! Talby!"

"What is it, Doolittle, what's the matter?"

Doolittle's face broke into a wide, Rabelaisian grin. "Guess what, Talby . . . I remember my name! I remember my first name!"

"Gee, that's great, Doolittle. I sure wish I could remember mine. It seems I've always been just 'Talby'. You're . . . you're lucky, Doolittle."

And that was it—he was lucky. He was going to die lucky.

"Hey, Doolittle."

"Yeah, Talby?"

"What is it? What's your first name?"

"Edward. Edward Vincent. Edward Vincent Doolittle." He sighed and felt completely happy. "Ain't that grand?"

"It's a beautiful name, Doolittle . . . Ed."

They were quiet then for a long time—several hours, in fact. Doolittle found himself drifting off to sleep. The sound of long, distant waves was in his ears, the cry of curious seagulls overhead, wondering at him sleeping on warm sand under his belly, when Talby's voice came over the suit speaker and roused him again.

"Doolittle . . . I'm moving out fast, Doolittle and . . . there's something else here with me. It's behind me, still in the distance, but coming up fast. Something that glows." Another pause and then, later, this: "It's a lot of things all grouped together, Doolittle. I can't describe it . . . a glow, radiation, internal light . . . but how they shine, Doolittle! I think it just might be the Phoenix, Doolittle!"

Doolittle roused himself sleepily and mumbled, "Phoenix?" He tried to turn himself, but no matter how he twisted his head, he couldn't seem to locate the brilliant apparition Talby was describing.

That was strange. He felt he'd covered every section of the sky. But there was no gleaming mass of "things" from outside. According to Talby's description, they should have dominated the heavens—if they were really there, that is.

Only it didn't seem to matter, now. Nothing seemed to matter. Edward Vincent Doolittle . . . how melodic. Melodic—no, symphonic! He heard it on his organ, played variations on it, piled fugue on fugue, made adagios of Edwards and scherzos of Vincents and great roaring Doolittle fortissimos!

What's in a name? Everything. What is a man but a measure of syllables?

If Talby saw his Phoenix, well, then he was glad for Talby. Yet it bothered him that he couldn't see it too. It had always bothered him that Talby seemed able to see so many things no one else could.

But he liked the astronomer in spite of that. Talby's excited voice cut in on his thoughts.

"It is . . . it's got to be, Doolittle! The Phoenix!"

"That's fine," Doolittle agreed encouragingly. He *wanted* Talby to see his Phoenix. And who was he to say it wasn't there, brought along specially for Talby by his good buddies the stars?

Talby saw them, all right. Drank them. They were so bright the intensity should have hurt his eyes, but somehow it didn't. There appeared to be a pattern, a regularity of form to the asteroidal collage.

But that was quite impossible. Weren't they purely a natural phenomenon? Weren't they?

And yet it seemed, as he drifted closer, that the pattern took on a definite outline, forming clearly established planes and connections here, sides and walls there, all bound glittering together in an astronomical baroque conclave of gravity and light and color and—something else.

He tried to concentrate on the nearest element of the Phoenix, but here the light was strong enough to defeat him. Yet he was sure he'd gotten a glimpse, and that the object at the center of that incredibly intense luminary was something other than mere rock.

What else it might be he couldn't put a name to. Or was it simply that in the last stages of life he saw what he wanted to see instead of what was really there? A peculiar tingling ran along his nerves, and there was a pulsing in his temple. He felt like a man teetering on the abyss of a great revelation.

"I'm . . . going into them," he whispered into his headset. "I'm going to hit them, Doolittle."

He ought to be sensible and close his eyes, he knew. The radiation that must surely be pouring from the ever-nearing Phoenix would undoubtedly burn out his retinas forever, despite the heavy shielding of his helmet faceplate.

But what mattered that? He would be dead inside an hour anyway. And there was no pain, no pain at all Only that feeling of expectancy.

There was one last thing he had to do.

"Doolittle?"

"Yes, Talby," came Doolittle's ever-fading voice, distorted by static.

"Before we get too far apart and our signals go, I just wanted to tell you . . . you were my favorite. Of all the guys on the ship you were my favorite. I really like you, Doolittle."

Doolittle considered this. His own attention was focused on the rapidly growing world below.

"I really liked you too, Talby."

Something floated past his face-plate. He blinked, forced his nearly quiescent mind back to a semblance of sentience.

"Hey, there's more debris from the ship coming past, Talby." Several large chunks of corridor wall ambled leisurely past him. "They're coming right past me."

"I'm going into them," came Talby's receding tones.

And then the astronomer looked down and saw something that amazed him, twice amazed that he could still see. The red world appeared to be receding far more rapidly than before.

"Hey, Doolittle. They're taking me with them, Doolittle. I'm going with them. I'm gonna circle the universe. Hey, how about that?"

Then he looked down at his arm. Tiny motes of light like curious insects were dancing around the sleeve, and the bright suit material was glowing brighter, brighter, until it pained him to look at his own arm.

He looked further, down at his right leg, saw that it too was starting to shine like the miniature firmament of an incandescent lamp. And something—something was happening to his body. Something painless and passing strange—a space change, rare and beautiful.

"I'm with them now, Doolittle," he called. "I'll be back again this way some day." And then the change was complete, and he fell into that abyss of revelation and—knew.

"Doolittle, it's wonderful . . . Before it's too late, I

want to tell you. I know what the Phoenix is now, Doolittle, and I want to tell you . . . it's . . ."

Edward Vincent Doolittle watched fragments of the *Dark Star* parade past him, tumbling slowly.

What was it Talby had said there at the last, before his suit radio had faded forever? He didn't remember.

But it had been good, he knew that. Poor Talby, poor grand, gone, lucky Talby. Out of the ashes of the *Dark Star* at least one of them had been reborn.

And he—he had his name again. He eyed the debris and his gaze focused on one particular, unspecial piece. And perhaps—something more.

A slow smile started to spread across his face. A quick glance at the panel of miniature instruments inside his faceplate showed pressure outside—slight, but rising rapidly. He was in the outer edges of the atmosphere and falling fast.

It would be over very soon, but he still ought to have time.

"Talby," he called, unaware that the astronomer was completely out of range. Even if he'd been within range, the present Talby couldn't have heard him anyhow. But he called nonetheless. "Hey, Talby!"

The ladder would pass very close—the metal ladder that had once led from one level of the *Dark Star* to another. It would pass too far . . . no. He reached out and got a hand on it, pulled it close.

A long section of ship's ladder, straight and unbroken. It held steady as the two of them plunged planetward together.

"I've caught a hunk of junk, Talby, and . . . I think I've figured out a way!"

He'd been sitting in the water for hours now. Hours. It was evening and overcast and the wind was starting to get really bad. But the tourists had long since gone and even most of the regulars had taken their boards in, strapped them atop their cars and called it a day.

But at the last minute before sunset the red ball of the

sun had slipped under the clouds and now exploded over the mountainous horizon in a last warming burst of affection.

He knew it was out there. You had to be patient, that was all, and meet the vast open spaces on their own terms. Even so, they might play you false all day, all month, all year, forever . . . but eventually, if you were patient and played straight with them and bided your time, they'd come through.

And then he saw it—sensed it, rather—a ripple on the horizon coming toward him fast and strong, and he saw that he'd been right to stay with it, right to wait while all the others gave up and left.

Been right to go out far, farther than any of them, farther than all the waves broke, and then it was humping up like the back of a gray whale, sliding up out of the ocean toward him, stretching from point to land's end. It was a little wider at the crest now as it heaved up behind him, but it wasn't going to break early—it was going to be a good wave, a great wave.

A perfect wave.

He got to his knees on the board and bent forward and then, just at the right moment, he clawed furiously at the water. He was in such good position that he only had to paddle once. Then he felt himself being lifted up, up, in the palm of a green-gray-black God.

Up . . . and then he was on his feet, knees bent, arms outstretched for balance, sliding down the crest, hearing the thunder-wall behind him, hearing the shriek of air as the curl—big as a subway tunnel, it was!—overtook him and he settled in under the roiling foam.

He braced himself hard against it so the wind howling out of that cavern wouldn't blow him off the board, stayed upright despite the fact that it tore and screamed at him, a friction generating a heat he could almost feel through his wetsuit. A charring, raging, surging heat as he bent his knees and slid into the atmosphere.

Beginning to glow . . . seeing the ladder beginning to glow beneath his feet and his suit glowing too, in spite of the water turning a cherry red, and the air wave was upon him, suffocating him, tearing at him. But it didn't tear him down, even though he saw he wasn't going to make it—wasn't going to get out of the curl.

And even, finally, when his face plate cracked from the heat, his smile didn't because the wave was lifting him up, up toward the blue sky, toward the planet, up and over and down and under into the star-flecked, foam-speckled blackness.

Wipeout . . .

DEL REY *SCIENCE FICTION CLASSICS FROM BALLANTINE BOOKS*

CHILDHOOD'S END, Arthur C. Clarke	27603	1.95
FAHRENHEIT 451, Ray Bradbury	27431	1.95
HAVE SPACESUIT, WILL TRAVEL, Robert A. Heinlein	26071	1.75
IMPERIAL EARTH, Arthur C. Clarke	25352	1.95
MORE THAN HUMAN, Theodore Sturgeon	24389	1.50
RENDEZVOUS WITH RAMA, Arthur C. Clarke	27344	1.95
RINGWORLD, Larry Niven	27550	1.95
A SCANNER DARKLY, Philip K. Dick	26064	1.95
SPLINTER OF THE MIND'S EYE, Alan Dean Foster	26062	1.95
STAND ON ZANZIBAR, John Brunner	25486	1.95
STAR WARS, George Lucas	26079	1.95
STARMAN JONES, Robert A. Heinlein	27595	1.75
TUNNEL IN THE SKY, Robert A. Heinlein	26065	1.50
UNDER PRESSURE, Frank Herbert	27540	1.75